THEN UPON THE EVIL SEASON

Noel Virtue was born in Wellington, New Zealand, in 1947. He came to England in 1967 and for several years worked as a zookeeper with the London Zoological Society and as head keeper of the Welsh Mountain Zoo in Colwyn Bay.

Noel Virtue's first novel, *The Redemption of Elsdon Bird*, was published to outstanding critical acclaim. It was also shortlisted for the first *Sunday Express* Book of the year Award, the David Higham Prize and New Zealand's prestigious Goodman, Fielder Wattie Award. His third novel, *In the Country of Salvation*, has recently been published by Hutchinson in hardback and will be available in paperback next year.

Noel Virtue lives in Hampstead and is currently completing his fourth novel.

ALSO AVAILABLE IN ARENA BY NOEL VIRTUE

The Redemption Of Elsdon Bird

Noel Virtue

THEN UPON THE EVIL SEASON

ARENA

An Arena Book

Published by Arrow Books Limited
20 Vauxhall Bridge Road, London SW1V 2SA

An imprint of Random Century Group

London Melbourne Sydney Auckland Johannesburg
and agencies throughout the world

First published in 1988 by Peter Owen Ltd
Arena edition 1990

Printed and bound in Great Britain by
The Guernsey Press Co. Ltd
Guernsey, Channel Islands.
ISBN 0 09 967360 6

For my friends Edwin Peacock
and John Zeigler, of Charleston, S.C.,
in memory of Carson McCullers

I should like to thank Margot Thomson in New Zealand for her invaluable research and impressions of Opononi, the background for this novel.

1 Those Tiny Tykes

When Lubin Croft saw the orphaned dolphin for the first time he and his mum Effie had been living in the bach at Opononi for only a few weeks. Lubin's dad Adin had caught the TB back in Whangarei, so after he was dead Lubin and Effie had cleared out, once they had buried him. And since they had been living in Opononi Effie had become certain she had been joined by the missionary Gladys Aylward. She spent her days cooking rice and scrag-ends of meat, offering feeds to passers-by on Gladys Aylward's behalf. They had always had a queer sort of a life, but Effie and Lubin loved each other a heck of a lot.

Lubin was seventeen that summer. The friendly dolphin which locals had begun to call Opo was drawing people from all over to have a look. The place was chocka. Effie had wanted to come here for a bit of peace and quiet and to get away from their sticky landlord. They owed him a lot of rent. They had escaped from Whangarei in the dead of night. Piling everything they could into the jalopy, they had headed up the Northland. Adin had owned the bach at Opononi. Effie hadn't known about that until after he was dead. She had found the papers in his old rucksack along with a load of money. The money came as a good omen, Effie reckoned. There was enough to get them by for quite a while.

On the trip north they had crashed into a couple of fences and lost a huge number of Adin's tract, *A Joy to Walk with Jesus*. The boot door had fallen off the jalopy and the tracts had blown out. Effie reckoned she had heard a noise, but they hadn't stopped to look. They had discovered the damage and the loss only after stopping for a cuppa on a layby half-way up. It had been real stiff luck, Effie had moaned, to this start of their new life without Adin the Evangelist. She had been hoping for a better time.

Lubin was on the beach, watching the dolphin. He had been there for an hour. There were a lot of people dotted across the beach. Because it was still early in the day, there was a hush over the crowd. Some Maori kiddies had entered the water and the dolphin had swum into the shallows. The kiddies called to the dolphin in whispers. A pakeha bloke had been doing his block at them for being too rowdy. The sounds drifted across the water with an echo. All over Opononi there was a feeling of joy for the dolphin. People were shook by it all, just as Lubin was. He had never seen people acting like this even at a huge salvation crusade they had once been to, down in Auckland. Here he and Effie had come to live, miles away from anywhere, and jokers with wives and kiddies were arriving from all across the country acting smoochy with each other just because of some dolphin that hadn't the good brain to keep out of it, away from people. But Lubin was pretty biffed by it. As soon as he got back to Effie, he told her, 'It's a real dag. All these blokes with their wives carrying on like the dolphin was Jesus.'

'Don't blaspheme, son,' Effie said quietly. 'I don't like blaspheming just because your dad's dead. He wouldn't've like it. Whatever would my Gladys think?'

As she always did after saying aloud the saintly lady's name, Effie would stand erect and still with a dippy grin, as if she had pushed off someplace else in her head.

Effie came up only to Lubin's shoulder and Lubin was

small. Effie was getting pretty old now, Lubin knew that much. He reckoned she had more wrinkles on her face than there were shells on the beach. And it was getting to be like her friend Gladys Aylward lived with them. Still, Lubin loved Effie even more, now that Adin was dead. Lubin had loved Adin too with a feeling like pain that tore him up inside. Adin had preached love and salvation all over the country in all weathers. But when it came to his getting crook with the TB, Jesus hadn't lifted a finger to help.

Effie was standing at the stove stirring her buckets of rice. They had been eating boiled rice and scrag-ends of meat for weeks now. Effie reckoned it was what all those poor people in deepest China had eaten in the dark days, so it was good enough for them.

'Gladys is real happy about this,' Effie told Lubin. 'That lady was a saint. She has goodness in her blood. She was a martyr to the cause, a blessed servant to humanity. Those Chinese devils she loved should be grateful.'

On and on she'd yack. She'd carry on even after Lubin got out of the bach. It gave Lubin the pip sometimes, Effie's going on about Gladys Aylward. As if Lubin didn't count. It somehow made the pain of his dad being dead as sharp as a pin.

Effie had got Lubin to erect a trestle-table out in the front yard. To the table she lugged the tin buckets of rice and meat. She had tacked a sign to the bach wall. The sign read: *The Inn of Happiness*; and below that was written: *We have no bugs, we have no fleas*. She had copied it from a book on the lady that Effie believed had become her friend. Effie would sit behind the trestle-table holding her tin ladle. She'd wait for people to pass. She hoped to invite people in to stay the night after a good feed. 'Come ye who are heavy laden!' she'd sing out. So far she'd had no takers.

'I don't get it,' she told Lubin. 'All the starving tykes in this world and these people stare at me as if I'm a foreign devil with typhus!' She would whimper and scratch at her head a bit until Lubin held her. He'd calm her down. Sometimes when she got a bit shook over something he'd carry her to her room and tuck her into bed for a rest. She was so tiny, as light as a puffball now. She had lost weight. Because Lubin was seventeen and nearly full grown he had to make certain that Effie was all right. What Effie got up to was just a bit of a dag, he reckoned. Her way of not going bonkers after what they'd been through.

Lubin at seventeen looked like a Jesus angel, according to Effie. Unlike many teenagers he had an unblemished skin. He had high cheek-bones. Lubin had a grin that Adin had reckoned could open up Heaven's Gate. But the one thing that stole from his beauty was his left leg. It was shorter by inches to his right, and was withered. They had not been able to afford special boots for Lubin, as Adin had claimed. Most of Lubin's early life had been spent walking with a real crook limp. Eventually Effie had nagged until Adin had paid for special boots to be made by a cobbler in Auckland. Neither Effie nor Adin liked to ask anyone for help. They had always kept clear of the authorities. When they were crook, Effie treated them with potions and herbs that Maori ladies had told her about while they had been on the road. This was why his dad had battled with the TB, Lubin reckoned. Adin and Effie had been too stubborn to get proper help. But he loved them both. He had needed them all his life for what they had done to save it.

'Our Jesus sent you,' Adin had told Lubin since he had been tiny. 'He picked you out from all those lost jokers out there in our land and sent you to us. We've given you love that comes straight from the middle of our hearts.'

Lubin had often wanted to sling off at his dad for the way he'd yacked on. Adin had often talked to Lubin and Effie just as he spoke when he was preaching on the road. But to them he'd spoken gently. He hadn't shouted.

After tea Lubin sat amongst the belladonna that grew across the empty section joining theirs. He'd sit here because it was pretty cramped inside the bach. Effie's non-stop yacking to Gladys Aylward while she darned socks or did the ironing gave Lubin the pip. And after dark, possums would pelt all over the bach roof. They made a heck of a racket. The noise made Effie so wild she talked even more loudly to Gladys.

Lubin liked being on his own. He had got used to it in the past, when he had been a kiddie. Adin and Effie had been so stuck on each other that sometimes they'd pushed off alone together on the tandem bike Adin had bought off a farmer. Other times, Adin went off without Effie for days on end. They had been bad days and nights for Effie. She had cried non-stop until he came back. Adin never told her where he went, or what for. Effie had told Lubin that he'd shoved off alone for years, before Lubin showed up. She'd just had to put up with it. In those days there had been no car. Lubin had got used to being left behind once he grew too big to sit in the basket on the front of the tandem. He hadn't minded. They'd usually brought him back chocolate fish or some buzz-bars for being a good boy.

Amongst the belladonna Lubin sat and made up songs in his head. He liked quiet songs with words that made him shiver all over. They made him long for what the world out there might offer. Since he had turned seventeen he had felt a lot of songs inside him. It had got stronger since they had been in the Hokianga. Opononi was a real strange settlement. He reckoned there was something a bit spooky about it. Lubin sat there singing aloud to himself, once he had made up some words. Effie sat on the bach steps. While she listened to him her eyes watered like anything. Effie liked having a weep. But she'd weep from Gladys Aylward's eyes, from her heart and from her sorrow. That stopped Effie from missing Adin. In front of Effie marched all the grinning Chinese kiddies that Effie's friend had walked to freedom, across China. And when it had got late but before Lubin came inside to boil the jug for Milo, Effie dried her tears and crept inside to her bedroom. Lubin would find her there, kneeling beside her bed in prayer. Lubin would stand with his grin that could open up Heaven's Gate. He'd tiptoe out into the kitchen to make their bedtime drinks. Lubin would grin to himself because their new life so far was a bit of all right.

Opo the dolphin was making the settlement a famous place. Lubin began leaving the bach every day before sunrise, to join in what was going on. Before Effie woke up he got dressed and tore down to the white sand beach where people gathered on the shoreline. The crowds now collected there earlier and earlier. It was not far off Christmas. A lot of people spent time on the road before and during the big holiday shut-down. Hundreds headed for the beaches. This year Lubin reckoned they were all coming up to the Hokianga. Photographs of Opo were in the national newspaper almost every day.

Lubin kept away from the crowds. People stared at him. Lubin was someone that people stared at. Those staring eyes were sometimes chocka with feelings that scared Lubin. So he kept to himself. When he reached the top of the beach there was a sharp tang in the air he could taste. Faces glowed and the sea looked like a huge stage. The sun was already a bit fierce. All these people, the way Lubin saw it, were watching the water like they were waiting for a miracle. He wasn't so keen on getting close to the dolphin, it was the faces he liked to watch. The faces made him come out in goose-pimples. He sat amongst the tussocky grass and the toetoe, grinning at the giggling, shouting kiddies. They were pelting across the road on to the white sand, now that the sun was up. Each one of the kiddies, Maoris from a nearby Marae and pakeha kiddies from the motor camp, waded into the sea calling 'Opo!' When the dolphin appeared and leapt out of the water, she would get cries of welcome and wonder. Lubin was transfixed, sitting there on his own. Fretting how he could get Effie across here so she could have a good look too.

Lubin noticed a bloke staring at him as Opo frolicked in the shallows. Lubin hadn't seen the bloke around before. He didn't look local. He wasn't wearing shorts. Lubin stared back after a few minutes. The bloke stood very still with his head turned Lubin's way. His face was the only face looking in Lubin's direction. It started to make Lubin a bit fidgety. The eyes weren't too friendly. There was no smile. Lubin looked away, picking out Opo's shape in the water amongst all the kiddies surrounding her. When he glanced back, the bloke had moved. He was walking straight towards Lubin, real fast.

At the same moment Lubin heard someone behind him, far off, yelling out his name. It was one of the Maori boys he'd been friendly with, called Pita, tearing across the marram grass flats. Lubin got to his feet, one eye on the bloke and one on Pita. Pita's face was twisted with effort as he pelted towards Lubin. He was yelling out, 'It's Missus Croft, Missus Croft. She's felled!'

With Pita pulling at him, trying to get him to go faster, Lubin ran in his jerky, lopsided way across the marram grass, heading home towards the bach. He didn't look back.

13

People were crowded along the paling fence that surrounded their yard. Part of the bach roof right at the edge had collapsed.

'It's your mum. She felled off the roof!' Pita was shouting in Lubin's ear. 'She's got hurt!'

Effie was lying on the dry earth. One of her legs was twisted under her. Her eyes were shut tight. Lubin could see that she'd wet herself. Some bloke tried to hold Lubin back as he started to yell out and push at people to get them out of the way. Lubin bashed out with his arms and knocked the bloke down. He threw himself across the fence, falling heavily on to his side. He scrambled over to Effie on his hands and knees. When he reached her he tried to push some ladies away who were standing over Effie fanning her with their skirts. Lubin yelled, 'Get away from her. Mum, Mum!' But suddenly he saw stars and he conked out. Everything went as black as pitch in his head and he fell down on to the earth like a rock.

Two teenage holiday-makers rushed Effie off to hospital in the back of their Bradford van. There was no ambulance anyone could call. One of the ladies had been inside and found a few of Effie's things, to send along with her. When Lubin came to, he was sitting propped up against the bach steps with a blanket over him. A lady was trying to pour hot tea into his mouth. Lubin had got the hiccups. The lady was saying, 'It's the shock, it's the shock.'

Lubin pushed her out of the way. The tea splashed all over her frock as Lubin tried to peer past her into the yard. Effie was gone from sight. The lady told him that his mum had been taken off to a hospital. Lubin started to yell out. He turned his head in all directions looking for Effie. He began to swear and hit out at people around him. Everyone got real quiet. The yard was packed with people now. They just stared at Lubin as if he'd lost his marbles. On a few faces there were looks of pity. An old bloke came forward and started patting Lubin on the shoulder. Lubin doubled over, hiding his face and eyes with his arms. He got quiet, but only for a minute.

'She'll be right, mate!' a bloke called out a few minutes later. 'She's not flipping dead. Calm down!'

Lubin started to rock backwards and forwards. His head was still hidden. One of the ladies reckoned he was about to throw a fit. And the sound he started to make caused all of them to back out of the yard, thinking they'd got a bit of a loony there in front of them. For as he rocked, Lubin was keening at the top of his voice and he'd begun to hit at his legs with his fists, and he didn't stop doing that for a full five minutes.

2   Call Me a Crook Mother

Effie and Adin Croft found Lubin as an abandoned baby
in the bush, inland from the Ninety Mile beach. The little
tyke had been dressed in a frilly pink frock and the note
that was pinned to his blanket read: *Please love my baby
girl. Jesus bless the good people who do.*

Effie and Adin had been travelling the north. Adin was
handing out religion to people on the outer, hoping
they'd hand him some money. Astride their tandem bike
with pannier-bags and a pup tent tied to the handlebars
they'd heard the baby crying one night while they were
off the beaten track looking for someplace to camp.
Finding the baby shook them both. Yet it gave them joy.
They reckoned right then and there that the baby had
been sent to them so they could become a real family. Of
course it wasn't made easy when the authorities got to
hear about it. Adin wasn't too keen to report the discovery,
but Effie reckoned he had to. The whole business dragged
out like a mile of red tape. It had made Adin all the more
determined that the baby should become part of his and
Effie's lives.

A country-wide search was carried out for the little
tyke's mum while he was kept in care. Adin acted like a
true battler to get him back. When all the hoity-toity
jokers who knew best had spouted their opinions off,
and no trace of the baby's mum was found, after a year
Adin and Effie were allowed to adopt him. By that time
the pair of them had settled down. Adin had become a
respectable Church minister. That went down all right.

16

They were renting a decent home and acting morally good. It was a personal triumph for Adin. He'd battled long and hard, he reckoned.

So the little blighter whose mum had reckoned him to be a girl became Lubin Croft, with one withered leg shorter than the other and a new dad who was a minister and a mum so tiny that behind her back she was sometimes called a dwarf by wicked tongues. The house they had lived in then was a two-bedroomed weatherboard on a small section in a town called Cambridge, south of Auckland. Adin and Effie had a good sort of life, but all Adin saw about them were people growing greedy. Sin was becoming just a bit of a dag. The Hell-fire that Adin had always warned of and the fear of it that he had tried to put into others, which was his living, was not thought much of any more, the way he saw things. His living was threatened. Effie once reckoned to Adin with a grin that it must be all the sinners passing water on to the Hell-fire, putting it out, which let people enjoy fornication and adultery and avarice with relish. People seemed to booze far more. There were public houses springing up all over the show. Adin had given her one of his frowns that could be pretty scary.

'There will be no forgiveness when the trumpet sounds!' Adin would spout from the pulpit. 'He will not be mocked. He will not forget the sin He sees amongst you! I see it, brother. I see it, sister!' Outside church Adin was loving and protective and stuck on Effie. He was a different person when he wasn't being a minister. Adin was tall and thin, with a gaunt face below his black woolly hat. He was rarely without his hat. Most of the congregation were scared stiff of Adin Croft. Yet he worshipped and cherished Effie and became so stuck on Lubin when he came into their life. Their early life together was chocka with hope. But it was no sooner than Lubin had learnt to walk and talk that Adin, taking Effie and Lubin with him, got back on the road again. They left the Church life behind. On the front of the tandem Adin built the wire-mesh basket in which Lubin sat as they travelled. Adin made a cover so their sunbeam wouldn't get wet or sunburnt. They had put their furniture and the boxes filled with *A Joy to Walk with Jesus* into storage. For some time they biked round the North Island. Adin preached and converted and relied on kindness for food and beds if he couldn't get money off people. Though they were pretty poor most of the time, they got by. It was during those years that the love grew between the three of them, a true and powerful love that meant more than the preaching did to each of them. On the road and free as they were, their love formed into something precious, Effie thought. They were, most people reckoned, a pretty odd family. Adin so tall and Effie a tiny dumpling, and Lubin even then a beaut little boy, with his white, blond hair that didn't darken as he grew, and huge green eyes. The difference in the length of his legs, the short one being so shrivelled, caused a lot of ladies and a few blokes to get pretty choked when they saw him. It helped Adin get more money in his collections. Adin and Effie always made it plain to everyone that Lubin was adopted. They told Lubin as soon as he was able to get the message. Effie hadn't been able to conceive. 'There's something dicky about my womb,' she had explained to Lubin when he was six.

'What's that, Mum?' Lubin had asked.

'It's where babies grow from. The Evangelist would've put some seeds into it if it wasn't crook and a baby would have growed there. But my womb's all cranky. It's twisted.' Effie took hold of Lubin's tiny hand and held it to her stomach. Lubin bawled his eyes out. He often cried when he heard upsetting news. 'It's where you would've come from if you'd been our real kiddie,' Effie

18

carried on, after hugging him and wiping away his tears. 'But we love you more because you were sent to us. We found you up north in the bush just like weeny Moses in the bulrushes. Call me a crook mother, Lubin, but I am your mother, you know, your very own. The Evangelist, he loves you too just like I do.'

Those early years were pretty kind. They had no worries. Effie and Adin had the gumption to do things right for Lubin, in their own way. Though during those years they shifted a heck of a lot. Adin owed rent whenever they left any town or settlement but felt no guilt over it. He wasn't paid a proper wage for saving people who battled with Hell-fire. He took collections and egged on big hearts who showed generosity.

They didn't always camp out in the tent that some bloke had donated. They would get a house. Sometimes they'd stay with kind people, paying a bit of rent when they moved in. But Adin made certain that they never went back to a place twice without a long gap in between. They usually ended up owing money. He saved money from the preaching collections, telling no one. He didn't tell Effie for a long time, but she worked out what he got up to. As they moved about and when they did stay put for a while, the love each had for the other became blessed. It became precious, for they lived a cut-off life, despite the preaching.

Sometimes in the city they were treated like real back-blockers. They were giggled at or slung off at when they walked together. They didn't like city people much. It was then that Adin got the idea of writing lots of other tracts to follow *A Joy to Walk with Jesus*. He reckoned he'd make a bomb out of it. With money he collected from preaching he'd posted hundreds of copies of his first tract to people all over the country, asking for donations. He did pretty well out of that. The tract was a prayer, a song from the soul which Effie reckoned was so bonzer the words biffed out from the pages. The words made her eyes water like anything whenever Adin read them out loud in front of hotels and picture-show houses. 'Lift up our eyes to the grace of our heavenly dad, that we might hear the cicadas in the bush and the slaters on the earth praising His name! Come to Jesus, sinner, He hankers for your soul!' read the opening words. Adin would sell copies to anyone he met, or try to. The money helped them get by. The tracts had been printed for nothing by a good keen bloke in Wellington. Whenever Adin wanted more, they would be sent to wherever the three of them had got stuck, just as soon as Adin wrote to ask.

In those days Effie had privately pined after being an evangelist herself. She kept that a secret. She wouldn't have wasted her time in New Zealand preaching to Maoris and pakehas, she reckoned. Effie couldn't see that they needed as much comfort as the poor devils overseas she kept hearing about. She would have gone off to China or India to preach. New Zealanders were living off the pig's back, even better off than the people in the Old Country, from where most New Zealand pakehas had run away.

When the evangelist Billy Good Man came out from America to hold crusades in all the big cities, Adin, Effie and Lubin, heading off after him, were pretty taken by a huge set of meetings held at Eden Park in Auckland. Adin hired a caravan for them to stay in. It had attached to it a real modern chemical toilet. They stayed put for weeks on an empty section. They had got permission. Adin did his darndest to meet Billy Good Man. He was hoping to get some good tips off him about the preaching life. He almost managed it. Effie helped herself to flowers from front yards, pinching them after dark. She made corsage after corsage, which she delivered to the huge marquee for the gospel singer Ethel Waters, who was touring with Billy Good Man. Effie was dead certain that

Ethel Waters wore a corsage on stage one night. Through the months after, Effie grew to reckon that was true. Years later, in Whangarei, she read a book that Ethel Waters had written about her life. Ethel Waters became one of Effie's heroines.

Adin, with Effie and Lubin, walked down the aisle three nights running to get born again. Though Adin had been pretty browned off that he hadn't got close enough to the evangelist to get a grip of his hand or ask him for tips. It was the only reason he had tried three times to get saved, for he reckoned he was already saved.

Preaching in the streets in New Zealand the way Adin got his living wasn't common. There was a lot of slinging off. His Bible bashing wasn't liked much in some areas. Churches sent their own missionaries overseas to China or India. They went from door to door, cadging money. Adin always felt a bit shook at that, a bit brassed off at the competition. Yet he reckoned he didn't have total claim to handing out salvation and the right answers. He always gave his money's worth when he preached. He always fretted that he didn't really have it in him to be a competitor for converting. Despite the money it dragged in. The way some fishers of men bashed right into the Maori people whose land was being taken from them left, right and centre, as their own beliefs were, to be replaced by cheap housing and hymn-books, began to make him a bit bitter after so many years. Adin's grandmother had been a Maori. Her daughter, Adin's mum, had run off to live with a Dutch sailor, leaving Adin with Grandma. Adin's mum stayed with the sailor in sin until she had died of venereal disease. That had been the reason for Adin's own convictions when he grew up. His mum's past. In Effie, when they met, had been an innocence he had never found in other women. The feeling hadn't been squashed even after he discovered that Effie was barren. It had caused his love to deepen.

21

He had begun to put Effie first, though he carried on preaching for the money. He tried to love the people they lived amongst despite their good-natured sinning. He ruled the roost at home, and kept Effie and Lubin away from anything that might harm them. He made all the decisions. 'I love you more than I love the preaching life,' he'd tell Effie when they were alone, before Lubin was sent to them. 'You make my heart swell. In your eyes a light shines so bright, it leaves all about me cold and grey.'

Effie would smile gently up at him, the love in her own heart shining out. She thought Adin was a real man. He was so strong in his convictions.

Yet despite this love and their beaut roaming way of life the business of having to be like everyone else, to conform, became heavy by the time Lubin was old enough to be noticed. His interrupted schooling, and the fact that Adin and Effie did not keep a proper home in which to raise him, caused them to meet troubles all over. Then, eventually, they were tracked down. Adin and Effie ended up in the Law Courts. There was a threat of Lubin being taken from them because of rent owed to landlords and money owed to shops. They were forced by authority to knock off the gypsy life. Blokes turned out from all over to spout against them, in court. They would have to bow to the authorities for a while, Effie and Adin reckoned.

They were settled down in Whangarei in a small house beside a huge cemetery. Adin had been given a proper job there as a digger of graves. Money was taken from his pay-packets to help correct his debts. There were hundreds of pounds owing from all over the show.

Effie was more narked than Adin at first at how she and her two battlers were looked on by others in Whangarei. Some thought they were cracked. Effie protected Lubin from as much of it as she could, as that

22

was her job. The three of them managed to get along all right, living apart from people as much as they could. Adin worked hard at his job. But it was his being denied a life on the road that brought on the unhappiness and grief and the TB. Or so Effie reckoned. Effie kept Lubin out of school as much as she dared. She and Adin taught him in their own way, at home. Lubin wanted to be with them more and more as he grew. The only time they didn't feel brassed off was in the evenings, when the three of them were together. Effie and Adin would sit at the table carefully writing on envelopes. They wrote out names and addresses taken from telephone directories they had pinched from various towns. They were planning to send off copies of the tract, asking for big donations, so that one day soon when they got back on the road they'd have a fair few bob to spare. By then they'd had their furniture sent up from storage in Cambridge.

Lubin would sit up straight at the table, with a jar of flour and water paste. He'd dip his brush in it and carefully seal each envelope. Adin and Effie wrote and folded and stuffed. Lubin would sit with only his blond head in sight above the table surface. His tongue would stick out as he helped. While the three of them worked, Effie sang hymns. Adin would practise sermons. He'd tell stories about the Maoris. Effie reckoned his stories were real beaut. 'You should write a book!' she'd sing out.

Lubin would sit there with his grin that could open up Heaven's Gate. Looking over the top of the table from Effie's face to Adin's and back to Effie's, Lubin pasted the envelopes. In Lubin's grin and in Effie's eyes, and in the way Adin looked at them both, there seemed to be some sort of certainty. That they'd always be together like this. Because just as His eye was on the sparrow, it was on them, and love graced their hearts.

3   Lubin Alone

Because of her fall from the bach roof, Effie had been stuck in a hospital at a nearby township for two weeks. Lubin was hankering for her to come back. He had just waited for her to come back each day, at first. He sat outside the bach, staring down the road. He reckoned she wouldn't be gone for long. There had been no word from her. Just a message telephoned to the hotel about where she was and that she was all right. For Lubin not to worry. Lubin had been too scared to try to visit. Adin had taught him that hospitals were places people were shoved into when they were about to hit the bucket. Lubin spent the time shook with worry, hiding when the lady from the Four Square grocers came to see if he was all right. He kept finding food left on the porch. Trays of whitebait fritters. Savaloys in batter. One morning there was a huge pavlova covered with passion-fruit pulp sitting on the steps.

The settlement was now full up with people. Lubin stayed indoors with the blinds pulled down. It kept the heat out as well as any staring eyes. Long after midnight he crept out of the bach and headed down to the beach. Even there, people were camping in caravans, having come to look at the dolphin. His trips out were short. Lubin felt eyes staring at him from caravan windows. He felt alone and a bit scared. He started to fret that Effie was dead just like Adin was dead. That the authorities had kept the body and not told him about her dying. But as each new day passed, he hoped that someone might come with good news about Effie. He tried not to think about what they had run away from, back at Whangarei. He was shook at how easily Effie had seemed to push it aside. She'd loved Adin more than he had, he reckoned. Lubin never stopped thinking about what they had done, to ease the Evangelist's pain.

He sang his songs once the light had gone from the sky. He cried a bit for his dead dad. He fretted about who his real parents might have been. Feeling bad that they had just biffed him into the bush like a bag of rubbish when he was a baby.

Early one morning Lubin woke up too scared not to get to the hospital to find Effie. He decided to set out for it before dawn. He locked everything up and left the blinds pulled down and took Adin's rucksack with him. In that he put some of the wrapped food which had been left for him, with a bottle of fizz. He had a good idea which way to head. He set off quietly, singing some of his songs. He walked inland, away from Hokianga harbour. He knew it'd be a fair way and wasn't that certain of the proper route, so he stuck to the main roads, passing along them as quickly as he could and speaking to no one. Not trying to cadge a lift, he crossed farmland and dusty roads and rugged paddocks covered with cows, the thought of finding Effie, of bringing her home, egging him on. He had tried to use the jalopy, but for some reason the engine wouldn't tick over and he'd given up trying to crank it.

The land he moved through held some of the most unspoilt scenery in the country. Lubin didn't take much notice. Then, as he left Opononi, he spotted the bloke who had stared at him on the beach the day of Effie's fall. The bloke was coming out of a huge farmhouse set well back from the road. He didn't notice Lubin. The bloke was lugging buckets filled with something heavy. The land surrounding the house covered a fair few acres.

25

What made Lubin hang on and stare were some sheds and what looked like makeshift cages dotted about the place. As Lubin watched, hidden behind a clump of flax, the bloke moved from shed to shed and to some of the cages. He entered each one for only a minute. There was an eerie quiet. It was just starting to get light. Fog lay across the earth. Lubin could hear faint sounds like animal cries. After a while the bloke went back inside the house, slamming the fly-screen door. Lubin carried on walking down the road. As he walked, he couldn't get his mind off what could be on that land. He saw the bloke again in his mind, as he had first seen him on the beach, the look on his face that had made Lubin feel windy. He remembered clearly now because Effie's fall and her being taken from him had been all he had thought about for days.

By the time he got to the township and had found the hospital, Lubin was stonkered. He was hot and sweating and a bit brassed off. He sat beneath a Norfolk pine in the grounds, looking up into its branches. After a while he fell asleep. One of the hospital porters woke him. In a real unfriendly voice the porter told Lubin to push off out of it.

'I've come to see my mum. Mrs Croft. She's a patient, mister,' Lubin said.

He was taken across the grounds, shown his mum's ward and told he had only a short time. Visiting hours were almost up. Lubin began to feel a bit crook as soon as he entered the building. There was a strange pong everywhere he didn't like. He'd half reckoned he wouldn't find Effie.

When he did see her, grinning at him from a bed far down the ward, he stood still for a minute. He started to cry. Effie was calling out to him. Her voice cracked, her face was puckered into a queer grin that hit Lubin for six. He ran like the blazes down the ward towards her.

He ignored some bloke in a white coat shouting at him. Reaching Effie's side he threw his arms round her so roughly she shrieked, but then they both began to laugh. A nurse came over and pulled screens round Effie's bed. Lubin carried on holding Effie to him. He rubbed his face against her hair, breathing in her smell of lavender that he loved.

'They keep shoving huge pricks in me,' Effie whispered to him when they'd calmed down. Lubin sat on a chair beside the bed, holding her hand. 'They won't leave me alone, they ask me queer questions. A doctor bloke looked at my personal bits the other day,' she said, her face scarlet. 'I don't like it here, Lubin. I don't. I feel like a lump of dirt. Gladys won't come in. She left me. She stays out there, outside that window. I see her peeking in. I want to come home, I want the Evangelist. Why hasn't he come?'

'He's gone, Mum. Dad's dead, remember? He's not with us, he's up in Heaven,' Lubin whispered.

'Oh yeah, I forgot.' Effie stared at Lubin intently, watching his face, reaching out with her hand to touch him.' We mustn't ever let on, Lubin,' she said softly. 'We can't ever tell what we done for Dad. No one must hear of it. They wouldn't like it, we'd get it in the neck!' Effie's face twisted until Lubin held her again. It was as if they were the only people in the world. 'I miss him, son,' Effie whispered, her mouth opening wide in pain. 'We'll never see him again. You and I won't get to Heaven.'

'What the heck were you doing up on the roof?' Lubin asked her.

'I reckoned people might see me and come in for a feed if I was up there,' Effie said quietly. 'Thought I might get some kiddies to come. Gladys reckoned it might work. She said she'd spotted a Chinaman down the road. He might've had some kiddies.'

'My legs are only a bit crook,' Effie said after a silence.

27

'I'll be good soon. Nothing busted, ay! They're all rude people here. They don't want to hear anything about poor Gladys stuck out there in all weathers. I asked them to go out and hand her a brolly. She stands there all sopping when the dew falls.'

'You mustn't talk about her, Mum,' Lubin told her. ''Struth, they'll shut you up in the bin if you keep going on. They'll think you're a loony.'

'I'm not!' Effie shouted. Then she clapped her hands over her mouth. The two of them began to giggle, then stopped suddenly as if someone close by had shouted at them. 'There's a lady here who's had her leg off,' Effie told him in a loud whisper. 'She keeps asking where it's gone, what the blighters have done with it. Give me back my leg, you buggers, she keeps shouting!' Effie went scarlet when she realized she'd sworn. 'The food's all pongy, the vegies are rotten. When I say anything, they tell me not to sling off. They say I should be grateful for kind mercy. That matron's a nasty piece of work, I'm certain. Her eyes are too close together. She sucks her teeth when she stares at me.'

'Did they say when you can come home?'

'You'll have to ask for me. They don't tell me a thing. It isn't right. Ssh!' Effie froze as a huge woman in a blue uniform with a face Lubin reckoned looked like curdled milk came barging through the gap in the curtains.

'Well,' said the woman, 'and who do we have here?' As she spoke, she smiled and looked Lubin up and down. She spoke with a plummy English accent.

'He's my boy Lubin, Matron,' Effie said. 'He wants to take me home, ay. He'll look after me better. He's a good boy, he's blessed.'

'It isn't up to your son to decide, Mrs Croft,' the matron told her, not looking at Lubin again. 'It's up to us to know what's best for you, isn't it? Now then, we will have to ask this young man to say cheerio for now, won't we? It's time for our bath!'

'You ask him yourself,' Effie said loudly. 'I'm not going to. He's my boy.'

'I'll leave you to say goodbye, Mrs Croft. I don't want any more fussing from you. A bath is good for us, isn't it? It will help us get well!'

The matron left them alone. She marched out through the curtains, pulling them back so swiftly Effie jerked in fright. 'Boy, she's a cranky old biddy!' Lubin whispered.

Effie giggled, clutching at her nightie. 'She'll have heard you, son. She's got ears like a blinking elephant, that lady.'

Lubin got to his feet. Leaning over the bed he hugged Effie and kissed her on the lips. Her face got sharp and pinched when he pulled away. They didn't speak and didn't say hooray. Lubin was certain he had to get Effie out of the hospital as soon as he could. He had no idea how. He'd need the jalopy. He looked back as he began to push through the ward doors. Effie sat with her hands covering her face.

Once he had left the building, he peered through a window near Effie's bed. He tapped on the glass. Effie turned her head towards him just as the matron barged into sight and stood staring. Lubin gave Effie a huge grin. Then he drew up his hands. He pulled his lips wide open with his fingers and stuck out his tongue, crossing his eyes. Effie went scarlet and hid her head under the bedclothes. Lubin didn't wait to see the matron's face. He ran off as fast as he could in case she barged out after him.

A light rain was falling as Lubin walked off down the road away from the hospital. He just kept on walking, eating some of the food. There were a few cars about, but he didn't try to cadge a lift. It took him a long time to return across country to the bach at Opononi. By then the sky had cleared. The rain clouds had shoved off.

29

Once he got back, Lubin spent a few hours fixing the guttering where it had been wrenched away from the roof by Effie's fall. He strengthened the corrugated iron. He was so stonkered, after a while his eyes got sore. And he was so cold he cut his hands on the nails that stuck out from the roof struts. There was no one about. Dark had fallen. He worked quietly, so that in the morning there'd be no reminder for Effie of her fall, when he brought her home in the jalopy. He'd manage it somehow. There was no way he could let her stay in that place. He was scared stiff at the thought of returning to the hospital to rescue her, but he was even more scared about her remaining there. He should be looking after her here, where the two of them had got away from authorities and trouble.

Lubin cleared out the bach. He swept the floors and dusted. He went out and picked flowers from front yards of darkened baches, putting them in old jam jars beside her bed. Effie loved and cherished flowers. When he had finished, he stripped off and ran hot water into the bathtub, lying down in it with a huge sigh. He stayed there until the water had got cool and the steam was gone from the room. Over the settlement the night had lulled people into sleep. There were cries of mopokes and scrabbling of possums on the bach roof, but here inside the bach it was really quiet. Yet Lubin couldn't get to sleep after his bath. He sat beside Effie's bed and thought of her. He thought about Adin. Soon he was bawling his eyes out.

By the time the morning's light came through the window Lubin reckoned that he had to get the jalopy cranked up and working. He'd tear back to the hospital once it got dark. He'd rescue Effie. He'd have to figure out how. It might be a stinker getting Effie past that old biddy of a matron. He and Effie would have a good laugh about it afterwards. Gladys could even join in if she was still about. In the night he'd reckoned that Effie was all he had. She was the only person in the world that he cared about and fretted over, now that his dad was dead. He knew Effie would be thinking the same thing in her hospital bed. Lubin's heart ached for Effie's voice. It ached for her love.

Lubin was bashing away at the old jalopy engine after breakfast when he began seeing the motor bike. At first he just listened to it and didn't take much notice. Then, looking up, he spied it careering across the intersection a hundred yards away. Minutes later the bike would roar back again. Whoever it was on the bike was staring in Lubin's direction. The bike appeared, then went off and reappeared quite a few times. Because there were no people about in this part of the settlement, Lubin started to get a bit windy. The bloke on the bike was wearing a lot of clobber even in the heat. Lubin was certain he was being watched. The bike slowed down now each time it crossed the intersection. The bloke's face was hidden by a visor. Lubin thought he'd seen the bike before. A huge ancient job painted green, with spoked wheels. When he didn't hear the bike again after it seemed to conk out, Lubin got to his feet, staring down the road. He heard seagulls squawking above him. Voices were coming from the beach, where it seemed everyone on the settlement was gathered, looking at Opo. Here where Lubin stood beside the jalopy was a creepy quiet. Even the cicadas weren't making their usual racket.

When the lanky figure appeared, standing on the road, the morning's light seemed to darken just a bit. The figure just stood there, its arms hanging down. It stared straight at Lubin. The face was still hidden. Lubin felt his legs starting to shake. He stepped away towards the bach door. The figure, covered from head to foot in the biking gear, began to walk slowly along the grass verge. Lubin turned and ran. He pelted inside, shutting and bolting the door behind him. He knew why he was acting the sook. He remembered the green motor bike now. It belonged to the Whangarei landlord.

Lubin held his breath and crouched down behind the door, his ear to the wood. He couldn't hear anything except his own breathing and the beating of his heart. He waited. His nerves got tight like wires.

Lubin yelled out when he heard footsteps behind him on the kitchen lino. He hit his head as he twisted round to look. The landlord had barged in through the open back door. He stood there staring, his helmet and visor removed. His small black eyes looked wild. Lubin slowly got to his feet. 'Good day, Mr Griff,' he said.

For a while the landlord just watched Lubin. Then he said, 'You've gone as white as a frigging sheet.' His voice was cold. He didn't smile. Lubin had never liked him. He spoke in a mean, riled voice. 'Feeling guilty, ay? I'll bet. That's you, I reckon. Bloody guilty. Where's the old lady, son? We got business.'

As he spoke, the landlord fumbled in the pocket of his leather jacket. He pulled out an object and biffed it down on to the floor at Lubin's feet. The landlord watched Lubin's face. Lubin kept his eyes lowered. His face felt hot and sticky. He stared at the object lying on the floor. It was Adin's fob-watch.

The bach was very quiet. In the distance Lubin could still hear voices from the beach. They sounded joyful. There was a sound of country music. Lubin bent down and picked up the watch. He slid it into the pocket of his shorts. Bits of earth were still clinging to it.

'Dad must have lost it,' Lubin said. 'Mum'll be pleased. It's only worth a few bob though, ay?' He tried to sound calm. He even grinned a bit.

The landlord didn't grin. He just carried on staring at Lubin's lowered face. 'Bullswool,' he said. 'Frigging bullswool. You know where that came from, where I found it. I saw you wretches do the whole thing. Thought you'd hide up here in this dump? I knew how to track you, I knew about this place. Haven't gone to the coppers yet. I want my bloody rent money first. Your old lady owes me hundreds. You get it, sonny Jim, cripple boy, hundreds. She coughs up or I drag in the coppers. I'm putting on the acid, get it, should've done it ages ago. Where's the old lady?'

He stepped towards Lubin and begun shoving him. He started to slap Lubin's face, cursing. Lubin was thrown backwards. He tripped and fell, bashing his shoulder against the edge of the wall. The landlord reached down, grabbing Lubin by his shirt, raising the helmet up high, about to hit Lubin with it, yelling at him. In a sudden scurry Lubin shoved himself sideways, got to his knees and pushed forward, grabbing hold of the landlord's legs. He shoved as hard as he could. Lubin shut his eyes tight as he felt the landlord letting go. Lubin heard him falling away, giving out a cry of shock, the sound of his feet staggering across the lino. There was a dull crack and a long sigh and then a throaty rattle.

Lubin opened his eyes. Then his mouth opened too and he reckoned his heart stopped as he looked. Because the first movement he saw was a trickle of blood growing larger as it flowed across the lino. The blood came from the landlord's head. His head had hit the oven. There was blood on the edge of the oven. Lubin got to his feet. He stood there very still for a long time.

'You all right, Mr Griff?' Lubin called out after taking a step towards him.

The landlord didn't answer. There was no movement from him. The blood made a pool as it spread. It was a real bright red. Lubin stepped across the kitchen. 'Mr Griff?' he whispered.

There was still no reply.

Lubin crouched down, a foot away. His eyes were riveted on the blood.

4 Gladys Shoves Off

There was a full moon shining as Lubin rattled off down the deserted road in the jalopy. It was well after midnight. The sky was chocka with stars. With the moonlight so strong Lubin left the jalopy headlamps switched off until he was past the Four Square and the motor camp. There was no one about. The settlement was dead to the world. Lubin drove with his foot down. The jalopy shook and backfired. He'd finally got it cranked and ticking over sooner than he'd hoped. He was frantic to get to Effie. To get her out and bring her back so they could decide what to do next.

He had hauled Mr Griff into the front room and propped him up in a chair. Lubin had shut the front-room door and stayed in the kitchen until the day had gone and it was almost dark. There hadn't been a sound from the landlord. Now more than ever Lubin needed Effie and he was hanged if he could wait any longer. Lubin's hands were still shaking as he headed along the back roads. He tried not to fret about what had gone on inside the bach, what it meant, intent as he was on getting to Effie, trying to figure out how to rescue her. Everyone would be fast asleep, he reckoned. He was wearing sand-shoes and had brought a Balaclava to pull over his head. He wore dark clothes. He spied no one along the way except possums. He had to pull up a few times when the jalopy almost conked out completely. He had trouble with the steering. Once when he was parked beneath a group of pongas letting the engine cool off he yelled out at a sudden thump on the roof. A possum had fallen from one of the trees. When Lubin got out of the jalopy he could see the possum was dazed. Then it skittered across the roof and fell down to the road. It just sat there. When Lubin got the jalopy going, the possum still sat there staring. He had to drive round it.

He parked as close to the hospital as he could get. Pulling on the Balaclava and a pair of gloves, Lubin ran the rest of the way. It was now the middle of the night. There were deep shadows forming from the moonlight all round him. He reckoned he must look as silly as a two-bob watch, dressed as he was. He grinned a bit as he ran, thinking of what Effie might say when she saw him. He hoped he wouldn't give her too much of a fright. She'd have a few cracks to make after the rescue was over.

The hospital was pitch-black. A few lights were showing round the grounds. The gates were open. By the time he found Effie's ward he felt calm and ready to have a go. There was one light showing in Effie's ward. The light came from the end opposite to where she had been on his first visit. Lubin crept up to the window near her bed. He could see Effie straight away, wide awake and sitting up. As he went to tap on the glass, Effie turned her head. She looked straight at him and grinned. Then she waved. She was lipping some words at him. Lubin crouched there with his mouth open. She seemed to have known he was there before he had let her know. Her face was glowing, as if a light was being shone on it, but there wasn't a light on near her bed. Effie pointed towards the veranda door that stood to her left. She lipped more words that Lubin didn't get, but he got the message. Moving as fast as he could, bent double, Lubin pelted round the corner of the ward building. He tried the handle of the glassed-in door. It was unlocked.

By the time he had got through the outer sun-room

and into the ward, crouching as low as he could, Effie was sitting on the edge of her bed. She was grinning at him and wiping her eyes with a hanky. Lubin put a finger to his lips. He stared down the rows of beds. At the far end a nurse on duty was slumped across the table fast asleep. Beside her was an electric night-lamp. The nurse was snoring as loudly as a bloke. No one else in the ward seemed awake. Some of the patients were snoring too. Moonlight was spreading out across the floor. A voice grizzled, 'Hold me, Lilian.' Then it coughed and went quiet. Lubin gave Effie a quick hug before helping her down from the bed. Again he put a finger to his lips. Effie started to nod wildly. She showed Lubin that she could walk, but with a bit of pain. She had pulled on a large purple dressing-gown and slippers. Crouching down in front of her Lubin whispered that he'd piggyback her to the door. As he lifted her up, Effie started to snort with giggles. Lubin managed to piggy-back her almost to the door with no worries, Effie clinging on like a battler. But as he tried to pull the door fully open with his shoulder, Effie suddenly whispered loudly in his ear, 'Giddy up, gee-gee!'

Lubin nearly dropped her. He felt her legs slipping from his hold. When he struggled through the doorway, bent forward, Effie was lying across his back. Her dressing-gown and nightie had rucked up. They heaved across the sun-room floor to the outside entrance Lubin had left open. Lubin lowered her on to a wooden seat outside, where Effie sprawled, huffing and puffing.

'Hang on here, Mum,' Lubin whispered after he gave her a huge, smacking kiss on the lips. 'I'll get back for your things.'

'There's not much, I'm all packed up. It's under the bed!' Effie whispered back. 'I knew you were coming, son, I knew. Gladys told me!'

Lubin pelted back up the steps and into the ward,

again crouching as he went in, his sand-shoes making no sound on the the lino. As he neared Effie's bed he spied movement from the other end of the ward. In a panic Lubin slid on to the bed, yanking the sheet and blankets up over him. For a minute there was no sound. Then he heard a chair scraping back and a quiet cough. Slow footsteps came down along the ward. Lubin slid farther down into the bed. Covering himself completely he shook with fright, fretting that Effie might make a racket and call out to him. The footsteps stopped at every bed. He could hear the nurse breathing, he reckoned, as she came closer. Lubin felt his heart beating away. There was a strong smell of lavender on the sheets. Biting his lips, Lubin lay still until the footsteps faded back down the ward away from him. He shoved the sheet slowly down from his face and peered out. The nurse had stopped at her desk, her back to him. She was picking up a cup and saucer. Then she moved on, tiptoeing out through the swing-doors into the lighted corridor beyond. Without waiting, Lubin slid out of the bed on to the floor. At the same time he shoved two of the pillows down below the blankets to make the shape of a body. Effie's small bag was on the floor against the wall. Carrying it against him, Lubin crawled and shuffled backwards to the door, pushing it to behind him as he went through.

Outside, Effie was nowhere to be seen. Lubin felt crook with panic. A heavy fog had drifted down and with it a cold dankness. He called Effie's name as loudly as he dared. He squinted into the fog. Rushing forward he tripped over something in his path and went sprawling. He didn't get that it was Effie he'd tripped over until she shrieked. Lubin pulled himself upright and crawled over to her.

Effie was sitting up trying to rub her legs. 'I fell over!' she cried out. 'Gladys ran away! I was trying to chase her. She's got the pip over something, she just shoved off!'

Lubin gave Effie a piggyback all the way to the jalopy. The cloth bag with Effie's things was balanced between them and kept falling to the ground. The fog was now so thick they couldn't see more than a few feet in front. They were both stonkered when they finally found the jalopy. Lubin reckoned they must have walked past it a dozen times. After Lubin helped Effie in, she sat with her head resting back on the top of the seat, her eyes shut. She came to with a lurch as the motor turned over. The jalopy shuddered and then backfired.

'They've got all my clothes, son,' Effie said when Lubin got behind the wheel. 'I'm nearly in the nuddy. Hope there's no blokes about.'

The pair of them were quiet as they drove home. Lubin leaned forward, peering into the fog. The headlamps hardly cut through it. He had such a frown on his face that Effie reached out and held on to his arm. She kept drawing shuddery breaths and pulling the dressing-gown around her. Lubin felt her shaking from the cold. It took what he reckoned to be hours before they got to the road that ran through Opononi. By that time the coast breeze had thinned out the fog. Patches of mist lay low across the sea. Almost in sight of the bach the jalopy with a huge shudder conked out completely. Steam rose from the engine.

'You'll have to steer while I push, Mum. It's gone dry,' Lubin said after he had tried to restart the engine. For a while they sat staring at each other. 'Not far to go, ay, we're nearly there. I'll make some Milo when we get in,' he added.

'Gladys'll help push, son, ay. She's always keen to give a hand,' Effie said, grinning. 'She can shove like a good one, I reckon. She's a hard worker.' Then her face twisted and she stared about her. 'Oh heck, she's gone off. I forgot. She didn't say a word, son. She just tore off when she saw me coming. It was a bit queer.'

Effie was still yacking on about Gladys as Lubin climbed out of the jalopy. He stood waiting for her to move over into the driver's seat. She did after one look at Lubin's face. Huffing and puffing with the effort Effie sat clutching the wheel, squinting through the windscreen. She had to prop herself up, as the seat was too low. Lubin got the jalopy rolling, but only slowly. It took a lot of hard shoving before they could see the outline of the bach up ahead. No one was about as they rolled past the hotel. The motor camp was chocka with cars and trucks and caravans. There were more parked on every piece of spare ground. A hush lay over the whole settlement.

Lubin carried Effie from the jalopy. He was worn out from the shoving but scared stiff, now they were back, about what they might find inside the bach. He had pushed the jalopy until it was parked on the gravel out front.

Effie was wide awake now they were home. She was yacking brightly. 'They'll be sending out searching parties, I'm certain,' she said as Lubin carried her across the gravel and struggled to open the door while she clung to his neck.' They'll want this nightie back, and the dressing-gown. That matron lady'll be real wild! They were shifting me home anyway, son, so a nurse said. In the morning, I think. It was all fixed. They said I wasn't crook now, ay, just needed to rest my legs. It won't get them too het up. I left a note stuck to the wall telling them. I said I knew you were coming and thanked them for the feeds they gave me. The matron'll do her block!'

Effie was laughing like billy-o as they entered the bach, but she stopped dead when she saw what was propped up in her rocking-chair beside the sideboard.

They stood still, Effie in Lubin's arms, and stared at

the Whangarei landlord for a heck of a long time. Lubin didn't dare say a thing. Effie was dumb from the shock. The landlord sat as if he were still alive. His eyes were wide open and his corpse wore a rough bandage that Lubin had tied round the head to stem the flow of blood. The blood had seeped down and caked on the pasty face. Lubin plonked Effie down into a chair before his legs gave out.

'I didn't know what else to do with him,' Lubin said without looking Effie in the eye. 'He was out cold when I left, I think, but I'm certain he couldn't've been dead!'

'You've knocked him off,' Effie managed to say.

'I couldn't help it, Mum. He came at me like a loony!'

Lubin pelted across the room, yanking the candlewick cover off the settee. He threw it across the corpse without looking at it. Then he pulled out Adin's fob-watch from the pocket of his shorts. Stepping over to Effie, he placed it gently in her lap. He knelt down in front of her, blocking her view of the corpse. Effie didn't move. After a minute she looked down. She stared at the watch, her eyes getting huge until they lifted to meet Lubin's. Her face twisted into a look that choked Lubin.

'He saw us burying Dad, Mum,' Lubin said. 'He must have dug Dad up! I didn't knock him off on purpose, it was an accident, he fell. He was after money too, he said.'

'How did it happen, son?' Effie asked.

Lubin told her everything. His eyes moved all over the room. While he talked, Effie's gaze stayed on Lubin's face. The dark was now growing pale outside the windows. Lubin's face was pale too and drawn. It was drenched in sweat. Effie leant forward and pulled him to her when he'd finished.

'I didn't mean it,' Lubin whispered. 'I didn't mean to kill him.'

Effie shut her eyes tight when she saw over Lubin's shoulder that the candlewick cover had loosened. It had

41

slipped down from the head of the corpse. The dead eyes were looking straight at her.

It was more than two hours later when they decided to dig a grave out back in the bush and bury the landlord. Both of them reckoned it was the least they could do for him. It was quite simple, they'd done it before. And they couldn't drag in the authorities.

Lubin managed the digging himself with a shovel that was kept up against the side of the dunny. Effie couldn't help with the digging. Her legs wouldn't stand the strain. Lubin dragged the body out from where it had sat, across the grass and into the bush. Together they had wrapped a double sheet round the corpse. The sheet had blue flowers all over it. It made a nice shroud, Effie whispered. Effie held the tilly-lamp. She leant on Adin's old walking-stick which Lubin found for her. The dawn was still a long way off. They didn't talk and couldn't look at each other while Lubin dug the hole. After they had both lowered the body in gently and covered it with earth Effie knelt down. Lubin helped her. She recited the Lord's Prayer. After that they sang a hymn, to make the burial formal. Lubin stopped singing half-way through but Effie carried on, staring up into the heavens. Her voice cracked a bit. Lubin put his arm round her and held her after she stood up. Her legs were wobbly. Her face was damp and very white.

There were faint sounds coming from the motor camp when Lubin finished off pushing the earth across the grave with the shovel and pulling dead leaves over it. He had flattened the earth as much as he could, spreading the rest across the bush floor. Not far off people were stirring as dawn slowly appeared. Filthy dirty and too worn out to think about what they had done, Lubin busied himself blowing out the tilly-lamp which Effie handed to him, while Effie looked up into the sky. She was remembering Adin. Lubin could see that on her face. She was remembering Adin's burial.

The cicadas were already starting up their racket as the sun rose into the sky. From the beach they now heard voices. The voices called out. People were laughing. Lubin stood close beside Effie. She put her head on his shoulder. As they stared down at the grave, the sunlight grew brighter.

'His soul will've met his Maker by now,' Effie whispered.

5 From Saul

Effie's legs slowly got better. By Christmas Eve she said they were feeling bang on. They didn't talk about the landlord's burial. Effie couldn't face up to it. She'd given Adin's fob-watch back to Lubin and told him he could keep it safe somewhere. She did her darndest to pretend the whole thing hadn't happened, that she'd dreamt it. She cooked pikelets and nut brownies and a jam sponge she reckoned they could make out was a Christmas cake. Lubin had been down to the Four Square and brought back a small ham which Effie had already roasted, with pineapple chunks and cloves. They'd eat it cold. It was too hot to have Christmas dinner the way Effie would have liked. Christmas was going to be a scorcher. The bach ponged of cooking but it made them cheery. Their mouths had watered when they had peeked into the oven. Lubin had dug up a small pine tree from the bush and plonked it in a cut-down petrol tin, filling the tin with sods of earth. Effie cut up shapes from an old newspaper. She hung them on the tree, making one shape like an angel for the top. Just below that she hung the marcasite necklace Adin had given her long ago. The necklace was the only jewellery she owned. It wasn't much to look at now. Some of the sparkling pieces had dropped off and were lost.

'We've done a good job, ay,' she said. They stood holding hands, staring at the tree. They had placed the tree in the centre of the room. Effie lit the two candles sitting on the sideboard. They switched off the light.

'Gladys'd like this,' Effie went on. 'She didn't have much of a life across in that China country. Checking all those bound feet – heck, how they must have ponged! She shouldn't've had to do that job, poor lamb. It wasn't nice. She was a martyr. She faced loads of heathens in the gaol like a true battler, son. She stopped a riot all by herself. I wish she'd come back.'

'I know, Mum,' said Lubin. 'You've told me.'

After a while Effie added, 'The Evangelist is with us, Lubin. I can feel his soul in my blood. He's watching us, I'm certain. He understands, he forgives. He'd have wanted us to get by all right after he'd gone. He knew we'd have to protect ourselves.'

Lubin stared at Effie without saying anything.

Lubin had spent an hour out in the bush hiding the grave where the landlord lay. Along with the manuka scrub he had now planted there, he'd hauled a couple of boulders and plonked them on the earth, which he'd tried to flatten even more.

Effie reckoned she could plant bulbs there before the next spring. 'Some of those jonquils or daffodils, they'd be nice if we could get some,' she said. 'He was a nasty sort, so the flowers might help. It's a good resting-place, son. It's better than the authorities would've given him, I'm certain.'

They did not talk about why the landlord had come. There didn't seem any point, they both knew why. Effie did her darndest not to think about the death, or about what the landlord might have done, finding Adin's body. There was no question in her head that he had found it. They'd buried Adin with the fob-watch.

'The Evangelist's soul is up in the Mansions,' Effie whispered. 'It's not in Whangarei. We did what he wanted, what he asked us to do.'

45

Thoughts came to her at night. The thoughts made her cry out in fear. But Lubin would come running to her side. They would hug. He would sing one of his songs, with Effie in his arms, until she fell asleep, after they'd had a bit of a weep. So the nights, and the days, had passed by. Now, it was Christmas Eve. No one had come to accuse them. No one had come to herd them off to gaol for what they had done.

'Tomorrow is the birthday of little Jesus,' Effie kept saying. She was in the kitchen making herself and Lubin some tea. They were having sausages and boiled cabbage and a bit of the plum pudding she had made for the big day tomorrow. She had been able to scrub the lino in all the rooms and tidy the outdoor dunny just in case a visitor showed up. Not that they reckoned any would. Her legs had clapped out a bit after all the hard work. She had felt a bit queer while out in the dunny. She had sat there on the wooden seat for a while so Lubin wouldn't have to see her all shaky and drippy with sweat. The bach shone like a new button, she told Lubin when he came inside from checking the grave. She knew he was shook with worry about the grave. He was out there every day. 'You can pull off those mucky gumboots,' she added, 'and have a bath. You pong.'

Effie hadn't let on to Lubin about the man and the lady who had turned up a few days ago from the hospital. They had knocked on the door while Lubin was out. He had been across at the beach looking at Opo. Effie had hurried to the door thinking that it might be Gladys come back. She was beaming when she poked her head out. She almost shut the door when she saw it was two strangers. It gave her a real fright. The lady, who spoke first, was very posh. She told Effie they were following up her case. The lady wanted to know why Effie had just left the hospital like that in the middle of the night. They had brought Effie's clothes, wrapped in brown paper.

'The matron has been worried silly, Mrs Croft. It was a very thoughtless, inconsiderate thing to do. We were going to bring you home, you know, the following day. It was all arranged. You caused us a great deal of embarrassment, do you realize that? We could cause trouble for you over this!'

The man, who was wearing a suit and queer-looking glasses, had a beard. To Effie he looked like a sort of brainy professor. He didn't say a word. Every time Effie looked at him, he'd grin. His grin was so big Effie wondered how many teeth he had in his head. He seemed to have far too many. They didn't look natural.

'My boy Lubin came over in the jalopy,' she told the lady. 'He can drive, he needed me back here, it was urgent. I'm better off now. I've good pins. I left you a note. I'm very sorry for making trouble.' Effie felt a bit windy. Posh people always made her feel windy. Her mouth had gone dry.

'You must take care, you're still on the mend. We'll try to come back to see you in a few weeks, just to make sure, Mrs Croft. At your age one has to be careful, do you understand? You've been lucky, you could have broken that leg.' As the lady spoke, she didn't look Effie in the eye. Her eyes were jerking like organ-stops about the bach. The man didn't take his eyes off Effie. He stared and grinned and kept on staring. Effie wondered if he was all there. He might not be a professor after all. His grin made him look a bit of a dunce, with all his buck teeth, now she had got used to his face.

'My friend Gladys wouldn't of wanted you to come here nosing,' Effie said to them in a loud voice. 'She knows all about how to watch after legs and feet. She's done it a lot. I don't need the hospital. She'll look after me now, I'm certain. And my boy will. So you don't have

47

to come back if you get busy.'

As the two of them went to the door, the man spoke for the only time. 'Is your friend Gladys a nurse?' he asked, grinning his grin.

Effie saw that he sprayed as he spoke. She reckoned that he must have false teeth, that the dentures didn't fit. As he talked they clacked. 'Gladys is a missionary,' she told them proudly, and banged the door shut on them. So far, they hadn't come back.

Lubin had pelted down to the intersection when he had left the bach. He had told Effie he was going down to the beach to watch Opo, but he went to search for the landlord's green motor bike. It was nowhere to be seen. Days had gone by before he had remembered it. It had vanished. There was no sign that there had been a motor bike left there at all. He peered into people's yards and searched behind the hotel, where he hoped it might have been taken. He knew he had seen it, no mistake. On the way down past the beach, after, he saw the Maori boy Pita, who had come to tell him about Effie's fall.

'You seen a motor bike round here, Pita?' Lubin asked. 'It's a big green job. It's got spoke wheels.'

'Nah, don't know that one, I think,' said Pita. 'I haven't seen one like that. I'd of remembered a green job, ay. Is your mum still crook, Lubin?'

When Lubin said she wasn't and began to walk off, Pita sang out after him, 'Do you want to play some marbles?'

Lubin turned his head, shaking it. He grinned.

'Boy, I thought your mum'd been knocked dead, you know,' Pita added, yelling at the top of his voice. By then Lubin had crossed the road. 'I'se getting some butterfly marbles for Christmas. Bet you've not got none of them!'

Lubin headed down to the shoreline. The dolphin was

leaping up out of the water. A girl was chucking a red rubber ball. Opo was butting it. Opo was flipping over in the water, rolling the ball on her belly, flicking it with her tail. A huge crowd was making a heck of a din in response. Above them the sky was a pale blue. The sun was scorching. Lubin stayed there for two hours on the beach, watching Opo in wonder.

Effie and Lubin had just finished doing the dishes hours later and were waiting for the jug to boil when they heard a loud knock on the front door. It was pitch-dark outside and real quiet. They were going to have an early night and get up at the crack of dawn. Effie reckoned they should, as it would be Jesus's birthday. She had been fretting that she had no present for Lubin. She had racked her brain trying to think of something she could wrap up and put under the tree. In the end while Lubin was in the bathroom she had folded a framed photograph of herself and Adin into a sheet of newspaper and written on it: 'To my son, a Happy Christmas from his loving mother.' She had placed it under the tree so Lubin would see it. It was a photograph she loved and cherished. It was the only photograph she still had of herself and Adin together, taken just after they had got married. She eyed Lubin's face as he pretended he hadn't noticed the small parcel. He didn't say a word, but she saw he had spotted something there.

'It could be the coppers,' Effie whispered to Lubin as they stood still and quiet in the kitchen. The knock on the door didn't come again. 'Let's not answer, ay?'

'It's a bit late for the coppers, Mum,' Lubin whispered back. 'They wouldn't come at night, I don't reckon. It might be carol singers. I heard some were going round.'

Effie switched off the jug. They listened for singing voices, but all they could hear was a wind that had sprung up. It whistled across the bach roof.

After a minute Lubin whispered, 'They might've gone now. You hang on here. I'll have a look.'

Lubin tiptoed through from the kitchen into the front room. When he had gone, Effie stood very still and covered her face with her hands. Lubin unbolted the door and opened it. There wasn't anybody on the steps. But what was there made him step back and call out. Effie, expecting a nasty shock, hurried to his side. They stared at three parcels which sat on the top step. The parcels were wrapped in bright red Christmas paper. On each was stuck a small card. Lubin peered out into the yard and along the road. He couldn't see anyone. He bent down and read out loud the messages written on the cards. On two of them was scribbled 'To Lubin Croft, from Saul Smith'. The third card had Effie's name on it.

Lubin carried the parcels inside. He plonked them on the floor beside the tree. One of the parcels was pretty heavy. Effie and Lubin stood staring down at the red wrappings, feeling a bit windy.

'Gladys,' Effie said after a long silence. 'They're from Gladys, I'm certain. She's done it under a Bible name.'

'It can't be, Mum. You know it can't.'

'It's a good-wisher then. Someone who wants us to have a happy time. Because it's little Jesus's birthday,' Effie said. 'It could be a friend of Gladys, ay. She knew lots of people overseas. Some of them might've come over here too to help her out.'

It was an hour before Lubin said they should open the parcels and have a look. Effie had made a pot of tea. 'It'll be Christmas soon anyway, Mum,' Lubin said.

Effie stared at him and grinned. 'You got three presents now,' she told him.

Lubin gave her a big hug and a smacking kiss on the lips. 'Yeah, I know. If we had some booze we'd be all right, ay, Mum?'

'Lubin, that's wicked. Whatever would my Glad....' But then Effie went quiet.

Without saying anything more, Lubin picked up the parcel with Effie's name on it. He laid it on her lap. She was sitting on the settee. She wouldn't sit in the rocking-chair. The dead landlord had been in it, she said. She had covered the rocking-chair with a blanket and pretended it wasn't there. Her parcel was large and soft. It rustled as she squeezed it. 'I bet it's a dressing-gown,' Effie said, then started to giggle. 'That'll mean I got two, ay. One for Sunday, Lubin. That lady ... I mean the hospital, they didn't ask for their one back.'

Inside Effie's parcel was a cloak. It was made with feathers. It was lined with what Lubin reckoned must be real pink silk. The cloak had a high collar and a silver chain that drew the collar together. On the lining was pinned a note which said the cloak was made from Emu feathers. Effie was struck dumb. Her face got scarlet as she stared. Lubin made her put the cloak on. He did up the chain for her, getting her to twirl about the room. The cloak touched the floor. Its feathers were soft and seemed to float as Effie did her twirl. The cloak looked very old. Effie couldn't speak. Lubin saw that her eyes were watering. She stood there looking down at herself and stroking the feathers. Effie was stonkered for anything to say.

In the heaviest and largest of the parcels Lubin found what he thought at first to be a wooden suitcase. It had a brass handle, a brass circled hole in its side, and a brass lock. In the lock was a small key. Lubin opened it up.

'It's a gramophone!' Effie sang out. 'It's like one that Adin's mum used to have, all those years ago. Adin sold it when we got married.'

Effie showed Lubin how to lift up the needle-arm, how to screw in the motor handle that was clipped to the inside of the lid. Lubin was trembling. Now he couldn't speak. He picked up his second parcel and ripped off the paper. Inside it were four records in cardboard envelopes. There was no note, no letter to explain. He couldn't get why anyone would have given them such presents. He was stiff with fright about who it could be.

Then Effie said, 'Put this one on, son.' She spoke in a cracked voice, holding one of the records out. She had become as jittery as a box of birds. Effie pushed the record into Lubin's hands and she covered her face when he had taken the record off her. Lubin figured out how to wind up the motor and to put in a needle. There were two small tins of needles inside the gramophone. Lubin read the label of the record Effie had given him. 'His Eye Is on the Sparrow,' he read out loud.

'It's Ethel, it's Ethel Waters. That nice lady who sung at Mr Good Man's meetings in Auckland,' Effie said. 'I made her lots of corsages. She wore one at a meeting, I saw it. She sings like an angel. I read her book, Lubin. It had the same name as that record. She's the angel of my heart.'

Effie was trembling as the music and the song began. Ethel Waters's voice filled the bach. Effie began to cry from the words, knowing all about Ethel's life. Lubin put his arms around her. They sat on the floor now, beside the Christmas tree, and listened. They played the record over and over again until Effie worried it would wear out. They should save the others until it was morning and the birthday of Jesus, she said to Lubin. There were two Ethel Waters records, and two of Gracie Fields. Effie told Lubin she had heard about Gracie Fields. She lived in the Old Country and was very famous and had a bonzer voice. 'She's been on at the pictures, in a film. A lady at Whangarei told me about her. She's a film star,' Effie added.

Lubin stared at her face, wondering if she'd made that up. Though Effie never usually told him fibs.

52

'I always wanted to go to the pictures,' she said. 'Your dad wouldn't let me. He said they were a vice. Silly, ay?' She giggled and clapped her hands over her mouth.

Effie hugged the cloak, stroking it with shaky hands. Lubin studied the gramophone and the records. It was gone midnight when Effie reckoned they'd better get to bed. Lubin said he could open Effie's present to him in the morning.

'It's Christmas now, son,' Effie said quietly. She looked a bit hurt.

Lubin had a grin as he picked up Effie's present to him and unwrapped the paper. When he saw what was inside, he went quiet for a minute. Then he told Effie that it was the best present a son could have from his mum. Effie grinned with pleasure. 'You really want me to have it?' Lubin asked.

Effie nodded, but then she looked away from him. Her face twisted. Lubin reached out and put his hands on either side of her face, pulling her to him. He kissed the top of her head. Then they held on tight to each other, both a bit stonkered from what the night had brought. Both wondering who the heck Saul Smith was. If he were real.

Effie had taken off the feather cloak. She folded it carefully, putting it back beneath the tree. 'It's a Christmas miracle, son,' she said. 'It's Adin up above telling us not to fret about what we've done. He's got someone to send the presents, I'm certain.'

During the night Effie couldn't sleep, trying to figure out who Saul Smith could be. She got up six times to have a look out front in case the bloke came back. She reckoned he might have left the presents at the wrong doorstep and made a mistake over the names. He might show up and ask for the presents back. She got a bit nervy there in the dark. It didn't seem right, after what they'd been up to. They were being blessed from somebody they had never heard of. It seemed a pretty queer thing. 'Gladys? Can't you come back?' she asked into the dark, whispering through the open window. She didn't want to wake Lubin up. 'I'll be good now, Gladys, I promise. I've cooked pikelets and a ham for Christmas dinner. We've got a tree.'

But the night was quiet, and Gladys was quiet, and the sound of the sea was the only sound Effie could hear. She was too choked to say anything more, so she shut the window. The moon was hidden behind cloud and a sea fog was creeping in from the beach. She'd got goose-pimples on her arms from the chill.

After a while she crept over and stood in the doorway of Lubin's bedroom. He was breathing lightly. His arms were flung out across the bed. His face looked dark against the white pillows, he was so tanned from the sun. Effie caught her breath. He looked so beaut to her, just like a Jesus angel. She stood there for a long time looking down at the boy she loved so much, the only person in the world now she loved truly. Yet there was sadness in her heart. She was certain that she and Lubin were heading into a bad time. She felt it in her blood. The Evangelist wasn't there to put things right. Effie covered her face with her hands. 'We gave you your peace, Dad, just like you wanted,' Effie whispered. 'What will we have to do next?'

She walked slowly back to her bedroom. She reckoned the presents would have gone by the morning. She and Lubin had just dreamt about them. The dream would be blown to bits by the time the sun came up.

Christmas morning came with a blue sky and a fierce sun. Effie was woken up out of a deep sleep at dawn. A bunch of carol singers were passing the bach on the back of a lorry. They were belting out 'Silent Night'. Effie hauled herself out of bed after the voices faded. She pulled on her dressing-gown and went to wash her face. Lubin was still fast asleep. He was chortling, lying on his back, the sheet hanging over the edge of the bed.

Effie reckoned they'd just have to make the best of this Christmas, the first without Adin. She'd make certain it would be a bit of all right. They could play games. They could sing songs. For a while she couldn't look into the front room. Yet the tree with its gifts drew her there. Nothing had changed. The cloak and the gramophone and the records were still there on the floor. Ducking her head and grinning a bit she hurried off into the kitchen to boil the jug and get the day started. But as she went in she got a heck of a fright. She almost fell over and nearly cried out, but then she started to smile in joy. For kneeling down on the shiny lino, having a look into the oven where Effie had left the cooked ham, was Gladys, with daisies in her hair and a huge smile on her face as she looked up. And beside her, a beaut smile on her face, one hand on her hip and one reaching out towards Effie, stood Ethel Waters, in a real gorgeous frock.

6 A Good Sort of Life

Effie, Adin and Lubin had been living in the house back at Whangarei for some time when, after funerals had taken place, Effie would hurry into the cemetery and pinch fresh flowers from new graves. She would take Lubin with her and make a game of it, once the main gate was shut. Sometimes their poky house would get filled with lilies of the valley, red roses or carnations. She'd leave the cards behind, out of respect for the dear departed.

Adin had been one of four grave-diggers. He wasn't qualified, so he was paid less than the others. He'd done a lot of gardening as well as helping to carry out burial business. Adin had been put under an order from the Law Courts. He had to stay in the job and pay back all his debts. He and Effie had been told in no uncertain terms that Lubin was sure to be taken away from them if they didn't do right and make a permanent home. One bloke had reckoned that she and Adin shouldn't have been allowed to adopt him in the first place. Lubin was going to the local school. Effie had to be there for him when he came home.

'They don't reckon much of your dad and me,' Effie told Lubin. 'They want to keep us under lock and key. They really laid it on, those goody-goodies.'

It had all happened so fast, their being tracked down and stopped from living the gypsy life. Some bloke Effie couldn't even remember had come forward. He had started the trouble. He had got out some papers against them. Through a solicitor he had claimed that Effie and Adin owed him so much money for goods, he was going to take them to court to get it back. The authorities got involved and tracked Adin down. From then on it got worse. Other people showed up and reckoned they were owed rent too, and were owed money for food and goods bought but not paid for from all over the show. Effie and Adin had been pretty shook at what was said. They reckoned the kindness in people's hearts had died. The help Adin had given with his preaching was being forgotten. They were treated like real no-hopers. Someone even accused Adin of stealing. Nobody proved that.

Adin had always been a battler. With Effie by his side and Lubin in tow he had stood tall and steadfast while all the legal bashing went on. Most of it they didn't understand. There were so many hoity-toity spouters involved. The whole business confused Effie. For a while she reckoned Adin would get shoved into gaol. What for, she had no idea. In the end they were plonked like luggage into the Whangarei house. Adin was given his job as a grave-digger. They set out to try to act as they had been told to. It wasn't too hard at first. Pinching the cemetery flowers helped. It became a bit of a dag for Effie and Lubin. In those long days stuck in Whangarei living like everyone else they needed a bit of relief. They didn't have any nearby neighbours. Effie was thankful for that. The house overlooked a gully filled with bush on one side. On the other it faced the cemetery, so they were cut off. They didn't have to put up with any sticky-beaked neighbours. When Adin knocked off for the day and came home, and the other diggers had driven away in their cars, they had the place to themselves. Effie would have tea ready. Lubin would run to fetch Adin's slippers. After a bath Adin would sit tucking into his tea telling Effie about the job. People here seemed to die like flies.

Neither of them liked talking about the job. It wasn't a lot of chop, being a digger of graves. Effie knew that much. After tea, some evenings, the three of them would walk together. Holding hands, they'd wander amongst the gravestones. The cemetery was huge. It went on for ever. No one from town showed up in the evenings. The cemetery was a place where Effie found peace, with her two blokes. For Lubin it was a playground, a place of adventure. He and Effie would play hide-and-seek sometimes. Adin, sitting on one of the wooden seats, would watch and grin. Some evenings he'd join in and they'd end up laughing like billy-o. Once it got dark they'd walk slowly back to the house. Adin would sit Lubin on his shoulders and Effie would walk beside them, her arm through Adin's, peering up into their faces, the love in their hearts a special thing. The love kept them going during those years, as Lubin grew. His beauty became a thing that people would be open-mouthed about when they spotted him.

Effie would take Lubin off to the shops in the daytime, while Adin was hard at it. She would let Lubin stay out of school, as he didn't like learning. Effie had met his teacher and thought she was a queer sort. She was bald and wore a wig that she took off when she yelled at the kiddies. Lubin was scared stiff of her, along with all the others. 'Don't you let on about staying home,' Effie would whisper to Lubin. 'Dad needn't know about it, ay, it'll be our little secret.'

They'd grin and giggle together and plan what to do with the day. Lubin liked to go to the shops with Effie. She'd make it into a bonzer game. They'd look in shop windows holding a pretend hundred pounds and pick out what they'd like to buy. Lubin always picked out lollies and Effie picked out a nice frock. Afterwards they'd sit in the milk bar and have a meat pie each and share a milk shake before heading home. Effie would take

Lubin to and from the shops the back way. No one saw them. Down along a track that ran through the gully, they'd walk. They wore gumboots, as the gully was often wet. Some days they'd go to the library. Effie took home books about famous people. She kept up her reading about famous people for years.

Lubin got slung off at by the bigger boys in school because of his withered leg. He had a real bad limp in those days. Sometimes he'd come home starving because some big lout had pinched his sandwiches. He said he told his teacher but she didn't do much except yell and pull off her wig. Effie would get het up, but she kept clear of the school. Places like that gave her the wind-up. She made it up to Lubin by shouting him presents when she had a few spare bob – a box of balloons from Woollies, or perhaps a push-and-go car. Lubin loved cars even then. She made Lubin hide the presents so that Adin wouldn't think she was wasting money. In the end it turned out that Adin was also buying Lubin presents and asking him not to let on. Lubin's room got chocka with hidden things. When it all came out, they laughed like billy-o. Lubin shared a bag of black balls Adin had given him which Lubin had hidden in the wardrobe. Into the bag had crawled some slaters. Effie almost put a slater in her mouth.

Privately Effie reckoned that Adin had cottoned on to Lubin's staying out of school. He wasn't worried. They were just biding time. They'd clear out again soon, once people had forgotten them. They'd get back into the big yonder. Back on the road.

They had visits from officials. For a while a strict eye was kept on them. After a few years the visits grew less. The only person who came a lot was Mr Griff, the landlord. They didn't like Mr Griff, either. Effie had never liked him from the start, and Lubin was scared of him like he was scared of his teacher. Mr Griff was a cranky sort. He could turn nasty when he wanted. He had once asked Effie to let him root her. He had come right out and used the word. He had beaten round the bush a bit at first, as Effie hadn't cottoned on. He kept winking and she thought he'd got a crook eye. When he explained what he wanted to do with her, she went scarlet with fright. Mr Griff had showed up on days while Adin was far off on the other side of the cemetery digging a grave for a bloke who had been run over by a lorry while Lubin was at school. Mr Griff towered over Effie. He had ended up fondling her breasts and trying to get her to sit on his lap. Effie had yelled and ran to hide in the bathroom, locking the door. Mr Griff called out that he'd give her five pounds.

He tried it on again, but Effie wouldn't let him get near her after that. She'd given him a kick in the shins the second time. She'd wanted to kick him farther up, but missed. Mr Griff had called her a nasty name that Effie would never forget. She locked the front door whenever she spotted him hanging about in the daytime. Eventually he came only for the rent, at night, when Adin was there. Mr Griff would wink at Effie when Adin wasn't looking. The winking made Effie's stomach heave. It reminded her of how he smelt. Up close he'd ponged of BO.

The years passed by decently enough, but Effie watched Adin get quieter and quieter. He lost weight. He seemed to go off into a world all his own. Adin left her on the outer, as far as her heart was concerned. She tried so hard to reach the Evangelist. More and more often he wasn't all there. He would look straight through her. The pain in his eyes made her cry. Adin started to take days off. He'd tell his boss he was crook. He'd lie on the cot in the spare room.

Effie read books. She read about Joan of Arc and Florence Nightingale. It was about that time she first read about Gladys Aylward, and then Ethel Waters. As she sat reading her books she would listen to Adin in the spare room, coughing, until he fell asleep. He would stay up all night then. He'd pace up and down the front room while she lay hoping he'd join her in the marriage-bed. 'I love you,' he had whispered to her one night. 'I love you like I've always loved you, but my life is tainted. It's becoming black.'

Effie wept. She didn't really get what he meant. She tried to make him pack up. They could just clear out, she told him. The three of them could head off somewhere, go farther north. When she talked of the plan to Adin, he looked at her with his face gone scarlet. He'd say nothing at all.

It was soon after that, that he began to push off on his own again. He hadn't gone off and left her and Lubin for a long time until then. They had bought a jalopy from money Adin had saved, through a cheap deal. Now Adin would go away for days on end, alone. Sometimes he was gone for a whole week. Effie would have to cope not only with the pain that brought but with Adin's boss. His boss would barge over to see where Adin had got to and usually did his block.

When Adin came back he'd be choked with a sort of guilt. He'd be choked with love for her and Lubin. He would get back to work and come home on time and was cheerful. His cough seemed to disappear. They'd have their walks again in the evenings. And they'd sit at the table in the house, getting envelopes ready for sending out copies of the tract, asking for donations. There'd be joy between them. Yet it started to get false. The Evangelist was unhappy, and Effie knew it. He was restless. He was itching to get away again after a few settled weeks. Off he'd push in the jalopy, not saying a word about where

61

he was heading. Effie would bawl her eyes out until he came home safe. It began to happen more and more often. It went on for years.

'Where do you go?' Effie asked him once.

'To Hell. I go to Hell,' he whispered.

Slowly Effie began to work out why he was unhappy. She reckoned it was the life they'd been forced to live at Whangarei. And because she couldn't give Adin any kiddies. Adin didn't touch her now. Adin had spent most of his life on the road, and all this was suffocating him. But there was no blame in his eyes when he looked at her. They just carried on, heading towards that first evil season.

Adin worked hard digging graves and gardening. He laboured under the fierce sun and in the pouring rain. He was saving money, he told Effie, so they wouldn't be short once they cleared out. He told her quite a few times that he had a bit stashed away. Before too long the two of them were talking about when they'd push off. They could head down south to Wellington, get over to Picton on the ferry, try out life down there, seek out a new start. A good sort of life with their little sunbeam. He was now a teenager and thinking about the day when he could leave school. It frightened Effie that so many years had gone by.

'We'll get it,' Adin told Effie. 'We'll get that freedom back, away from where we aren't wanted. I could do the preaching for money. It was a good job that, Mother.'

Effie began to believe that was the truth. Yet within another six months Adin's hacking cough came back, worse than ever. He got so crook he started to stay off work again, and Effie made potions and syrups from her storehouse of Maori remedies. She nursed Adin while she waited for him to get well again. Then he was given the boot from his job, for taking too many sickies over a long period. The authorities were cutting back on staff,

Adin was told. Soon after that there was no money left for the rent and only a little Effie had put aside for food. Effie had no way of knowing how long it would take before Adin's health came back. She didn't seek help. They'd always kept to themselves. She didn't know how to change that. No one came to see them except for Mr Griff wanting his rent. He got nastier every week about it. They got letters, which Effie ripped up and flushed down the toilet before Adin spotted them.

Adin sat in Effie's rocking-chair during the day, until he got so weak from the coughing that he lay in bed. Soon it was Effie who slept on the cot in the spare room. Adin had the marriage-bed.

By this time Lubin had finished up at school. He was at home all day to help. Effie and Lubin kept talking about his getting a good job to see them through. Effie told Mr Griff about that one night when he came to the door. Effie hadn't let him inside since Adin had got so crook. Mr Griff wasn't even interested, said he didn't want to know. He just wanted his money, he'd keep on until he got it. He told Effie that if she did the dirty stuff with him now, all their troubles would be over. He'd chuck their bill out the window. Effie wouldn't listen to him.

Those days and nights went by as slow as a wet week. Somehow they managed. Adin got weaker. He started to cough up blood that looked black. Effie was shook with fear for his life. She wanted to get a doctor in. Adin made her say with her hand on the Bible that she wouldn't go behind his back. He didn't want a doctor. Effie panicked. One night when he was at his worst she pulled on her coat and hat to fetch someone to help. Adin climbed out of bed and grabbed her. He'd been so weak, he'd crashed to the floor. Effie hadn't dared to leave him. She didn't get why Adin was acting like this, now he was so crook. Yet she had always obeyed the Evangelist. She just hung on, washing him down when the blood came out and when he dirtied the bed, holding him when he called out for the Maker to take him to glory. For Adin reckoned that his hour was near. His mind wandered. Effie cooked herbs. She and Lubin force-fed the herbs to Adin.

'I've sinned,' Adin whispered to Effie. 'I've sinned so badly. This is my payment.'

Effie and Lubin sat together each evening after it was dark and when Adin was sleeping. In those last few days they did not leave the house at all. The three of them were left alone, as the landlord had gone up north. There was no one else. They kept the blinds pulled down and the doors bolted. Yet their love was still there, that didn't fail them, Effie knew that much. She and Lubin waited, and Effie had hope in her heart that her love and Lubin's love and her herbs would somehow get Adin well again. They could clear out to start the new life, down south, away from this place that had kept them shut up all these years. Yet in the end that hope had died.

'You've got to help me,' Adin had gasped on his last night. 'I've had it, Effie. It's over for me, I want to shove off now. You and Lubin can be beside me and send me home.'

He had coughed and coughed and the black blood had gushed out of his mouth like rotten meat. Effie with tears pouring down her cheeks had run to get Lubin from his room. They had sat beside Adin's bed, all three hanging on to each other's hands. Outside there had been a bright moon. There had been so many stars in the sky that Effie reckoned Adin's path to Heaven was being lit up. Adin told them quietly how he wanted it done, in between the coughing and the black blood and the pain that made his body heave. He said it would be real quick. It wouldn't take much, he told them. He was too worn out.

He was too weak to feel anything now. His death was waiting for him there, in the room. 'Too tired, too tired,' he whispered. 'No more battling.' It was the only way, he told Effie, smiling up at her face. They would be forgiven. He spoke to them for a long time, his voice getting weaker. He spoke to them for the last time as the Evangelist.

When he had gone silent, and while Effie sang a hymn, Lubin took a pillow and placed it across Adin's face. Both Lubin and Effie held the pillow down until Adin had died. He didn't struggle. When Lubin lifted the pillow, Adin was smiling. Effie leant down and kissed his lips. She held him to her for the last time. Effie sat beside Adin's body all that night. Lubin brought her cups of tea. She kept vigil most of the next day until it was again dark outside. She washed Adin's body. She dressed him in his Sunday preaching suit. She combed his hair.

Adin had made them promise they would bury his body, without help, in the private place they had decided on. He didn't want strangers to touch him. He didn't want the authorities shoving their noses in. He wanted all his things with him. Copies of his tract. His woolly hat. The fob-watch he had treasured. He said he didn't care about having some Church minister saying words over him. He was the Evangelist. His soul would be all right. Effie and Lubin could get back on the road after, as his soul would have gone from this place. There was no need for a coffin. Effie had wept bitterly at that. But he had always led them. Effie had always obeyed, for the three of them had shared love.

At night Effie and Lubin had laid Adin's body to rest out in the bush behind the Whangarei house. They buried his body in a secret place where no one ever seemed to go. They stood over the grave that Lubin dug. They recited prayers. They sang hymns. Lubin hid the grave so well that they reckoned no one would ever find

65

it. They'd done it out of love.

And before the week was over, Effie and Lubin were packed up and heading north, to the bach at Opononi, where the season of the dolphin had already begun.

7   Up the Booay

Christmas had come and gone. It was the new year. Effie reckoned they'd survived the old one just about, and this one couldn't get any worse. Christmas had done her the power of good, she told Lubin. Gladys Aylward had come back with the heroine of her heart, Ethel Waters, in tow. And now Saul Smith the animal man had showed up too.

Effie wasn't too stuck on him. He'd given her the wind-up when they had met. Saul Smith was a lot younger than she and he was a bachelor. At forty years old she reckoned he should be married, with kiddies of his own. Instead he mucked about with animals and wanted to build a circus. Effie couldn't credit it, anyone wanting to be with animals when there could be a loving wife and kiddies to be with and to bring up. All Saul Smith wanted to bring up were baby rabbits and guinea-pigs and strange birds. Saul Smith had turned up at the bach a few days after Christmas. He told Effie how he'd felt pretty sorry for them, hearing that she and her boy were on their own in a strange place. As he'd had some gear he didn't want any more, he'd reckoned the cloak and the gramophone and records would make good Christmas presents and cheer them up a bit. He'd been given the cloak by an Aussie. The feathers had come from loads of emus. Effie felt a bit suspicious at what this Saul Smith had done. But she had never understood human nature.

Lubin had taken to Saul from the start, this bloke who didn't really explain who he was or where he'd come from and why. 'Saul wants me to work for him,' Lubin told Effie one morning. 'Said he'd pay us. We need the money more than anything, Mum. We're nearly flat broke, no mistake.'

Saul Smith had asked Lubin to join him one morning a few days after he had come to see them. Now it was Saul said this and Saul did that. Effie got windier with worry over it than she let on to Lubin.

Effie had become pretty keen on Dorothy, who lived on Saul's land. Dorothy was a godsend to anyone who came across her, Effie started claiming. Dorothy cheered everyone up without any effort. Lubin brought Dorothy over to the bach while Saul was off fishing. He'd given Lubin permission. Saul wouldn't let Lubin go fishing with him, he'd said it was man's work. Saul Smith was paying Lubin to clean out his animal cages and mess about with pelicans and fur seals, not to go fishing.

Dorothy was a young female emu. She stayed in the bach yard all afternoon some days, before Lubin came back to take her off again. Lately Effie had started to let Dorothy come indoors, she was so tame. Dorothy would plonk herself on the kitchen lino and Effie would talk to her. It made Gladys and Ethel wild, Effie told Lubin. The girls didn't like Dorothy much. She kept pooping all over the show. But Effie reckoned she was blessed with these new friends, even if one of them was only a feathered friend.

Effie had been a bit sick with worry about money. There wasn't all that much of it left, so the idea of Lubin doing paid jobs for Saul Smith seemed the answer all right. Saul had acted a bit kind. He had been generous. He sent over food and even offered to paint the bach. The weather-boards were peeling from the sun. Effie had told Lubin to say no. Saul asked Lubin one day why didn't the two of them dig up the land at the back so Effie could grow their own vegies. They could start a market garden. They'd make a bomb out of that.

Effie had got pretty shaky and cold over the idea, thinking about the hidden grave. The one time Saul had been inside the bach he had stared at Effie with a queer grin that wasn't quite right to her. It was a big grin, but there was something in it that got her back up. The feeling faded after a while.

Saul acted the good, keen man, according to Lubin. Lubin got stuck on him. He couldn't wait for the mornings so he could pelt off and muck out the cages and feed Saul's animals. Saul kept them on a farm just outside the settlement. Lubin told Effie that Saul Smith had stared at him once on the beach, the day of her fall. Effie got shook over that, though she couldn't figure out why. Effie found herself on the outer. Lubin trusted Saul and she wasn't certain of him. But he was being kind.

After a few weeks she felt better about him. There were the girls, who had settled in, and there was Dorothy. They kept her busy. Effie kept hard at it making preserves with the fruit and the jars that Lubin brought home. They had enough fruit preserves to last them until next Christmas.

'Why don't we ask him over for a feed?' Lubin asked Effie. 'He's all on his own, he must get real lonely out there.'

Effie wasn't too struck by the idea.

'He wants to take you across to see Opo,' Lupin added. 'He doesn't get why you haven't gone. Everyone else is going.'

Effie stared at Lubin. 'You could take me,' she said. 'I'd go if you took me, son. Gladys and Ethel can come. They'd enjoy an outing, I reckon. Gladys was saying the other day she doesn't do much, and Ethel'd be game. I'd like it better if you took us, not Saul Smith. He's your boss. I shouldn't get too thick with him if I was you. He'll only bite your head off about something. I don't

69

want you fretting. We'll go on own, ay, just the four of us.'

Lubin was so biffed about Effie wanting to see Opo after not showing interest before that he didn't get the pip about what she'd said about Saul. He knew that Effie didn't like Saul Smith much. He tried to keep tight about him as much as he could.

Effie shoved some fresh lamingtons into a bag, with two bottles of Lemon and Paeroa. They set off after lunch. Lubin hadn't been needed at the farm. It was Saturday, his day off. Lubin made Effie use Adin's walking-stick and wear her flax sun-hat.

'You can piggyback me if my leg gets sore,' she told him, grinning.

'There'll be a heck of a crowd,' Lubin told her. 'You stay by me and you'll be right. It gets noisy on Saturdays.'

The settlement was swamped with people. Cars, trucks and huge buses were parked end to end on the road that ran along the harbour's edge. The buses had brought people in from all over. Everybody wanted to have a look at the friendly dolphin. Effie reckoned that half of New Zealand must be there, when they got near the beach. There were loads of kiddies paddling in the shallows, and just as many adults hanging about. They were all waiting. Opo had not turned up yet. She went off to feed farther down the coast sometimes, Lubin explained to Effie, at Koutu Point. It was where a couple of fishermen, and Saul Smith, also fished. 'She's an orphan like me, Mum,' he said. 'They reckon some bodgie shot her mum and she came inshore looking for her. Opo's found people instead.'

'You're not an orphan, Lubin,' said Effie. 'You're my own boy.'

Opononi was a pretty tiny place. The biggest building

was the old wooden hotel painted green and white. It had a veranda with steps leading right on to the road. The veranda was packed with people when Effie and Lubin passed it. The hotel was booked up for months ahead. It had never done so well. A post office stood farther along the road, and a bowser, where everyone bought their petrol.

'That place must be doing a bomb,' Effie reckoned, as they walked by, pointing at cars and vans queued up waiting for service. A Four Square store was near the bowser, and a milk bar. Not far off was the Memorial Hall, and the motor camp, in amongst Norfolk pines. That place was really chocka now, Lubin told Effie. There wasn't an inch left. And beyond the settlement, inland, were the bare hills, where lots of all sorts lived and where there was a Maori Marae. The area was pretty cut off. Now, to Effie, it looked like Karangahape Road in Auckland on a Friday night. People were careering all over the show. There were so many kiddies, her heart beat like anything as she watched them. She pointed them out. 'Can't see any China ones, though,' she told Gladys.

Lubin settled Effie on a small rise of sand a bit away from where most of the people were waiting near the water's edge. The beach was quite narrow when the tide was in, the water pretty deep. The sand was white. Its reflection made people squint. The sea was calm, like glass. Way out across the water was a peninsula made from high hills of golden sand. At sunset the sand-hills turned pink. Lubin told Effie that the Maoris believed the sand-hills were sacred. They didn't go over there much, but all the pakeha tourists had been piling over in boats to have a good look. There were supposed to be Maori canoes buried there. The famous Maori Kupe, who had discovered New Zealand, had landed there when he had arrived.

71

Effie watched Lubin's face. His eyes shone.

'Blokes in boats found Opo, Mum,' Lubin explained as they sat there. 'They reckoned she was a shark at first. They've only just worked out that some bodgie had been shooting at dolphins. Someone reckoned he killed the one that must've been Opo's mum, but they can't prove anything.'

'Yes, son, you told me. It's wicked,' Effie said.

She was acting a bit shifty, Lubin noticed. She was staring about the beach with a queer look on her face. He fretted that she might not think much of so many people being close. It was a bit nerve-racking for her.

'A Maori bloke called Mr Hene found the dolphin. She came up to his boat and played round it. One of his mates touched her. She kept following them back here from farther out. And she's been coming back, all friendly, every day.'

Effie watched Lubin's face as he carried on talking. His eyes continued to shine. His whole face lit up in a glow that tickled Effie's heart. She didn't get why he'd become so stuck on this dolphin. Everyone making such a frolic about it, it made Effie feel a bit windy. All these people here – there must be thousands, Effie reckoned. There were huge signs by the roadside now that read: *Welcome to Opononi but don't try to shoot our gay Dolphin*. And a sign asking that kiddies be allowed to get out to the dolphin first and for them not to be rough or too rowdy. There were traffic jams on the road. Effie didn't like the noise but could see the funny side. They'd come here for peace and to get over what had gone on back in Whangarei and they were lumbered with all this, as well as the dead landlord buried in the bush.

Everyone around them was acting so cheery and friendly. Strangers were saying hello to her and Lubin. They offered fritters and sandwiches and fizz drinks. Effie couldn't help but be pretty touched by what she saw. By the time Opo appeared she was on her feet with everyone else, watching and grinning like they were.

Entering the harbour were two tiny motor launches. Just behind, as the boats putt-putted closer to shore, Effie could see the dolphin. Opo was leaping up out of the water in a real joyful way. The crowd surged forward. There were cries of greeting and happiness. Kiddies were streaming into the sea, the adults hanging back. Opo liked kiddies more than adults. Effie clapped her hands. She even forgot that Ethel and Gladys were with her. She grabbed Lubin by the arm and hung on as they squinted over the heads of the crowd. A group of kiddies had formed a circle by joining hands in the water. Opo swam inside the circle and started to butt a beach-ball being biffed by a teenage girl. Lubin told Effie that the girl's name was Lynette. She was Opo's favourite of all the kiddies. She was a real nifty swimmer just like the dolphin. Effie suddenly wanted to get closer. Lubin was so excited, his face was scarlet. He helped her through the crowd. Effie was wearing sand-shoes and Lubin had kicked off his boots. In a few minutes they had both waded out into the water, so taken were they by what they saw. Effie rolled up the skirt of her frock as far as she could get it. She tucked it into her bloomers. Before she knew it they were in amongst all the kiddies, just standing there in the sea. The dolphin was inches away from them. Effie reached out in a daze and touched Opo on the fin as she slowly swam past. Effie was certain after that some electric had run up her arm as she made contact. One lady told her that Opo could heal the sick, just by being touched. Effie and Lubin were now in water almost up to their waists but couldn't have cared less. There was excitement all round them, yet it was a queer feeling, Effie reckoned. It was like reverence. She and Lubin were dumb from it.

After a few minutes Opo went farther off, swimming

73

beside the girl Lynette whom Lubin had pointed out. Effie suddenly realized where she was and what had just gone on. She started to laugh out loud in pleasure. Kiddies began surrounding her on all sides, grinning at her because her laugh was so loud. A Maori boy pushed his way towards her. He cried out, 'Missus Croft, Missus Croft, my name's Pita!' Before Effie knew it she was giving Pita a real big hug. She didn't even know how he knew her or why she was hugging him.

Pita came with them when they waded back to shore. Effie's legs were feeling a bit weak now and shaky. She was leaning on Lubin and then on Pita, and then there on the shoreline amongst all the adults stood Saul Smith. He was staring at them. Effie noticed him straight off. He wasn't grinning like everyone else. He was staring at Pita. After a minute Pita ran off. Effie spotted that Pita's little brown face puckered up before he ran away. He looked scared stiff. But the moment passed and she found herself back where they had been sitting. They were stonkered and sopping wet. Saul had followed them and stood, still staring, not even saying hello.

Effie collapsed on to the dry sand after pulling down her skirt from her bloomers. She ignored Saul Smith. 'It's a fair miracle,' she kept saying. 'All those kiddies and that creature! Lubin, she was so gentle, like a lamb.'

Effie began yacking away to Gladys and Ethel, telling them all about it. Saul stood a few feet off, watching Effie with a stiff frown on his face. When Effie stopped yacking Saul stared at Lubin without saying a word. Then he walked away. He was soon out of sight. Lubin felt a bit shook. Saul hadn't acted a bit friendly. He'd told Lubin he never came down here to the beach, he was too busy. Lubin fretted over the look on his face as he'd watched Effie. Effie hadn't taken any notice.

After about five minutes Pita came back. And there was Effie sitting on the sand, her legs sprawled out, soon surrounded by Maori kiddies and a group of pakeha kiddies who streamed over. They seemed pretty keen on getting close to her. Effie began yacking away non-stop to the kiddies, telling them all about Gladys Aylward and about Ethel Waters and her beaut singing, just like the angels. Lubin squatted on the sand. He reached over and took Effie's hand. He held on tight.

The two of them stayed there on the beach for an hour, after most of the kiddies had drifted away. Effie's face was red and her eyes were brighter than Lubin had ever seen them. He knew it had been the kiddies round her that made Effie's face shine. Even after Pita had gone, tears of joy were still running down Effie's face. She was holding her arms about herself, her face so happy Lubin hugged her, there on the beach. He kissed her on the lips with a huge smack. People stared. Neither of them took any notice. Effie seemed a bit choked, filled with some emotion, wriggling her toes in the sand. It made Lubin's heart thump like anything, watching her. After a while they tucked into the lamingtons and drank the bottles of fizz. They were starving. Then they headed home to the bach. Opo had long since swum back out to sea.

'It's the best time I've had for ages, son,' Effie was saying as they crossed the road. 'All those little sunbeams, I could've squeezed them and kissed them all over.'

And the only thing that upset the day was Effie's legs clapping out before they had crossed the road. She went sprawling, Adin's walking-stick flying from her. But some bloke stopped the traffic and so many people ran like blazes to help out that, after, Effie told Lubin she'd felt like a real lady.

Lubin worked hard at Saul's place every day except Saturday. He worked there even on Sunday. He had fretted that Effie wouldn't like it, but she didn't seem to worry. 'Animals don't know what Sundays are for,' she told Lubin. 'They need their feeding just the same. Anyway, we've left all the religion behind us. And we need the money.'

After a silence she whispered, 'I never really wanted all that Sunday spouting after years of it. There's more to life than that, ay? We've our new life now, even if we have been criminal. But don't let on to Gladys, she won't like me talking that way.'

Lubin stared at her. Effie looked away. 'You miss Dad a lot, don't you, Mum?' Lubin said.

Effie got stiff. Her face was shook when she replied. 'I do, son, of course I do. It's a bit like that lady at the hospital, the one who'd had her leg off. I feel like that. Life won't be so good without the Evangelist, I'm certain. He was always in charge.' She started to cry and covered her face with her hands.

Lubin wound up the gramophone and put on a Gracie Fields song, 'Sing as We Go'. That always cheered Effie up. It made her laugh out loud.

Soon it was tea-time. Effie cooked chops and boiled two bunches of fresh puha and there were feijoa preserves and custard for pudding.

On Saul's three-acre farm he kept two fur seals in a huge tin bath. In a cage lived two pelicans. There were rabbits, a few guinea-pigs and a group of goats. Hidden away in a huge shed he kept two kiwis and three keas. He made Lubin swear he'd not let on to anyone that he kept those birds. It wasn't legal to keep them. He was planning one day to start a sort of circus if he worked things right. He'd supplied people all over in the past, with animals he got off an Aussie.

Lubin realized pretty quickly that Saul was a secretive

sort. He acted kind and generous but he was mostly unfriendly, like he had been down on the beach in front of Effie. Saul spent only a short time showing Lubin how to do all the jobs and what food to use. He went off fishing almost every day. The seals and the pelicans needed fresh fish, he said. He didn't have a freezer or anything fancy. He didn't have enough money to buy fish all the time. 'I use gelignite,' he told Lubin. 'Quick way to get fish. The bastards just rise up to the surface after a blast. A mate down south supplies me when he gets it.' Then he laughed. Lubin reckoned his laugh was cold. 'That's something else you don't let on about, ay, boy,' Saul told Lubin only once. 'I'll be down on you like a ton if you do. The cops are out to get me, the bastards. I've a record a mile long, but I don't really give a frig.' After he said that he laughed even louder.

Saul didn't scare Lubin but he sometimes made him feel windy the way he stared with a stiff grin on his face. It was Saul's acting kind that kept Lubin on the job. And the money. The money wasn't much but it helped him and Effie. They were better off now than when they had arrived, that was for certain. And now they ate good food. Saul let Lubin take home vegies and fish from his place. And all the fruit Effie could bottle. Sometimes there'd be meat. Saul owned two rifles. He went shooting in the bush for pigs.

Lubin became keen on the fur seals. They were pretty tiny and needed a lot of fuss made of them. Lubin wondered if these were illegal too. One of the seals liked chewing on Lubin's boots. Lubin spent a lot of time with them. The smallest one sat in Lubin's lap on hot afternoons and fell asleep. No one came on to Saul's land, at least when Lubin was there. The place was cut off and quiet round the back. Saul kept his animals out of sight as much as he could. He told Lubin to do the same and to keep his mouth shut if anyone asked him questions down in the shops. 'There's a lot of buggers round here who'd turn me in,' he told Lubin without letting on what he really meant. 'They watch me, I reckon. I bet some cranky bastard's reported me. I want that circus one day, there's good money in animals. I don't give a monkey's nuts, and they know it. Frigging laws are a bugger, but I'll keep what animals I like. Going to train the bastards and have a real New Zealand circus with trained kiwis. I'll make a million.'

Saul had talked to Lubin a lot at first, but he got quiet after a week or so. Lubin learnt quickly not to ask Saul too many questions. Saul never gave out any answers anyway, he just stared. Saul had asked all about Effie. Lubin tried to keep tight but Saul kept asking. Now he knew a bit about Effie and Lubin's lives. Not about being in Whangarei, though. Lubin told Saul they'd come up from Wellington. Saul had stared and grinned queerly at that.

Saul told Lubin he'd given him the job because he was a cripple. 'Bit of a bloody bastard that, ay,' he said. 'A frigging stinker, if you ask me. No worries, I'm keeping an eye on you two from now on.'

Then he'd laughed, but the look on his face had got Lubin feeling real nervy. Yet there was something wild about Saul, something raw, that made Lubin feel a bit excited. He hadn't said a word to Lubin about his dad, or where he might be. Once he had asked about girls. Lubin said he didn't know any and went scarlet. 'You stay clear, mate,' Saul told him. 'Sheilas mean trouble, they flaming drag you under. I should know.' After a minute he added, 'But I bet you'll break more than one frigging heart before you're much older, even with that bastard leg.'

Saul went bright red, barging off into the farmhouse and slamming the door. Lubin carried on scrubbing out the concrete pond the two pelicans shared. Saul watched

Lubin from the windows of the farmhouse. The staring went on quite a bit. Lubin looked up several times and spotted Saul's face in one of the windows.

After a few weeks, when Lubin arrived at the farmhouse, Saul wasn't there. He'd be gone all day. He never told Lubin where he went. And as Saul had said he could, Lubin took Dorothy back to Effie at lunch-time most days. Wearing a halter that Saul had trained her to wear, Dorothy would stay at the bach when Lubin returned to the farm. Effie was becoming as stuck on Dorothy as she was on Gladys and Ethel.

Effie missed Lubin a heck of a lot when he was off mucking about with the animals. She didn't like it, but she was keen on the money it brought. Saul Smith didn't come to the bach as he had done that one time. He'd been so polite to Effie it had got her back up a bit. She was pleased he didn't show up again. She didn't like blokes kowtowing to her. She wanted them to act natural. Saul didn't act natural, he acted a bit greasy. Over the years, because she was so tiny, blokes and some ladies treated her like she was not all there or a bit delicate. And Saul had acted worst than most. He had been nosy about the bach. He had stared at everything. That had shook her a bit, as if he had been hunting something down with his eyes. She didn't trust Saul Smith. She kept tight about it in front of Lubin, for his sake.

Some afternoons if the sun wasn't too scorching, Effie would sit on the bach steps with Gladys and Ethel. Dorothy would stand beside them pecking at everything that moved. She wanted to be so close to Effie, she'd push herself up against her. Sometimes Dorothy leant so heavily against her that Effie would get shoved off the steps. 'You're a bit of a loony,' Effie would tell the emu. 'Isn't she a loony, Ethel? You tell her.' Then Effie would laugh.

Dorothy must have something wrong with her, Effie reckoned. She pooped a heck of a lot inside the bach, it wasn't normal. Effie was forever cleaning up the muck. Dorothy would peck at her head when Effie was on her hands and knees with the dustpan and a piece of cardboard she used for the job. Most days when Lubin had left Dorothy at the bach Effie got no work done. The emu followed her about. She wouldn't leave Effie's side. She tried to lean against Effie all the time. Or she'd rear up and push her chest against Effie, stretching her neck and peering down with a look that made Effie laugh out loud. When Effie laughed, it drove Dorothy barmy. Dorothy would tear off and run round in circles and then leap into the air. 'Full of the joys of life!' Effie would sing out.

Dorothy seemed to like the gramophone as much as Lubin did. Lubin played Ethel Waters's records, and usually Gracie Fields, as often as he could. They didn't have a radio. Dorothy would squat down by the gramophone and become dead still when she heard the music. Her beak would hang inches above the revolving record. Then after a bit her head would sway from side to side and her feathers would twitch. Effie couldn't credit it when that happened. 'It's like one of those exotic snakes,' she told Lubin. 'You know, when they play that Indian music. Like it says under those pictures in our *Wonder Book of Animals*. That bird's real taken by the music. She hasn't got much upstairs, but she loves that music!'

Dorothy towered over Effie, and the emu wasn't yet fully grown. Effie would sometimes put on the halter and take Dorothy for a walk along the road in front of the bach. It caused quite a stir. People stared with their mouths open. And when someone came up and asked questions Effie felt real clever telling them what Lubin had told her about emus and how they lived over in Aussie. Some people just stared as if Effie were cracked, but they didn't say anything nasty.

Effie hoped that what was done, was in the past, that their deeds were history, even if they had been criminal. The past could be shoved aside. No one knew about the grave out back. The future could be chocka with good times and friendship. They had to carry on the best they knew how, in memory of the Evangelist, because they had loved him so much.

Pita the Maori boy began coming to stare over the bach fence. He'd stand there for ages, staring and grinning shyly, his hands behind his back. Pita and Effie were the same height. She reckoned he had a real gorgeous smile. In a queer way Pita's smile reminded her of Adin. It made her fret a bit. She missed the Evangelist all the time and she grieved for him in her heart. Effie would point out Pita's smile to the girls when they peeked at him through the windows. It was a while before she asked Pita to come inside. After the first time, having made Milo milk shakes and given him nut brownies, Effie couldn't get rid of Pita. He started to come every day. He'd knock on the door. He began bringing over bunches of beet or puha and, once, a cooked mutton-bird. Effie didn't dare ask where that had come from. Pita said his auntie knew he came to see Effie. His mum had pushed off, to live in King's Cross, Sydney, he told Effie. A man had taken her and made her into a sort of model in Sydney. She hadn't wanted to take Pita with her.

That shocked Effie. 'Do you like living with your auntie, Pita?' she asked.

'Not much, I think. She's always busy making money. She works on a farm all day, ay. She doesn't mind about

81

anythink. I can do what I like. She knows who yous are.'

'Why aren't you at school?'

Pita looked sheepish. 'I do lotsa bunks,' he said and grinned. 'Teacher says I'se useless. I'se no worries, though.'

Effie began to watch out for Pita most days. He'd tear along to the bach from the shops. And in a while, during the days when Lubin was off mucking about on Saul's land, Pita began to bring a few other kiddies to see Effie. They were all Maori. There were a few girls, but most were boys. To Effie they all looked like angels. She herded them inside and gave them feeds. They'd play games – pin the tail on the donkey or blind-man's bluff. None of them seemed to have heard of them before. They taught Effie games they knew, ones with sticks or string. Pita brought along his marbles. Some afternoons the bach was bedlam, kiddies tearing about laughing like billy-o, Dorothy leaping about on the lino and falling over. Gladys and Ethel would stand by, watching. Ethel's songs would be playing full blast on the gramophone. Effie's girls never joined in the games. It made the smaller kiddies a bit nervy when Effie talked aloud to the girls.

'Who are them ladies, Mrs Croft?' Pita asked her. He talked to her more than the other kiddies. Most of the others were pretty shy, but they gave Effie some real beaut hugs. They giggled a lot with their hands over their mouths.

'They're my good friends,' Effie told Pita. 'Gladys is a famous missionary from the China country and Ethel's a bonzer singer.'

'Oh yeah, you told me on the beach. Wish I could sees them,' said Pita.

The kiddies would secretly look all over the bach for the girls, giggling. But even Pita didn't say much to her about them. Each of them was too polite. Though Effie overheard one of the very small kiddies telling another,

82

'They's spirits, I think. You've got to squint, then you might see.'

Lubin felt a bit jealous when he knew that the bach got full of kiddies every day while he wasn't there. But he liked the idea. Effie was acting so happy. He fretted that some of the mums or dads might show up and do their blocks. None had, according to Effie.

Weeks went by. The kiddies kept coming. They didn't show up every day. The settlement was just as busy, even though the holidays were over. People were still pouring along to see friendly Opo. Opo the dolphin was now very famous. Lubin took Effie across to the beach twice more, but they didn't wade out into the water. The sea got too crowded with noisy sorts. It put them off going.

Effie began cooking rice again, with scrag-ends of meat. She got the kiddies and the girls to help out. Dorothy took a liking to the boiled rice, once it was cold. Effie made two new signs. The signs read: *The Inn of Real Happiness*. She hung them outside the bach. One day they hauled the buckets of rice out on to a trestle-table and stood round taking turns holding the tin ladle. Effie taught some of the bigger kiddies to sing out 'Come ye who are heavy laden!'

The kiddies seemed to think it a real good game and couldn't stop giggling. One scorching afternoon one of them hauled along a garden hose from his dad's garage, screwing it on to the outside bach tap. They all cooled off under its spray. Dorothy went loony and ran in and out of the water. Even Effie joined in.

They were all having a grand time and laughing like heck when one of the mums turned up to take a few of the kiddies home. 'You can't bother the lady all the time,' Effie heard her say as the kiddies were herded out through the gate. The lady didn't speak to Effie. She gave Effie a real queer grin and looked away. After a while the others said they'd better push off home too.

Effie was left on her own with Pita and Dorothy and the girls. They sat on the back steps drinking ginger beer that one of the kiddies had brought along in milk bottles. The sun was still fierce. Effie got Pita to turn off the hose. It had been left behind and was still spouting water.

'Where's your dad, Pita?' Effie asked him, once they'd been sitting for a time.

Pita shrugged and looked sheepish. He turned his head away.

'Is he in Aussie too?' Effie asked softly.

'I dunno,' Pita said, almost whispering. He glanced at Effie out of the corner of his eye.

'You can tell me,' said Effie. 'Go on.' She gave Pita a hug.

Beside them, Dorothy was shaking one of her feet. She kept putting her foot into a puddle of water made from the dripping hose. After she shook her foot she'd put it straight back into the puddle.

'My dad used to live here,' Pita told her after a while. 'In the bach.'

Effie went a bit stiff.

Pita twisted round and looked at her properly. He was frowning. 'Missus Croft, do yous know him? He hasn't been here for ages. He wasn't here long. He's the dad of a few kids round here. My mum wasn't married to him. He just took her out a lot and preached at her a long time ago. I'm not a full Maori, ay.'

After a long silence Dorothy made a rude noise and wandered off to peck at something interesting on the grass.

Effie asked, 'What's your dad's name, Pita?'

'Mr Adin,' Pita said, still frowning. 'His name's Mr Adin, Missus Croft. He's a pakeha, and he's a preacher. Do yous know him?'

8   Effie Keeps Tight

It was a few days after Pita's bombshell. Effie still couldn't credit what he had let out. Yet she didn't know how the heck Pita could have got hold of that name out of the blue. And he wasn't a boy to tell fibs. She hadn't told him who she thought his Mr Adin was, and he didn't seem to make any connection. Yet Effie knew Pita was Adin's son. She tried to fight it and it didn't ring true in her head, but in her heart it did. Everything was beginning to tally, the more she thought about it.

'How many kiddies belong to Mr Adin?' Effie asked Pita.

'I dunno. There's a few, I think,' Pita said, squinting at her in the sunlight. 'My mum lived here for a while, ay. She kept the bach neat when Mr Adin wasn't around. Mum was his best lady, she told me. And Mr Adin didn't give her anythink for the cleaning. He was a bit of a mean bugger.' Then Pita blushed, having sworn. He hung his head.

Effie didn't sleep for nights. She said nothing to Lubin about it, but she told Gladys and Ethel, and Dorothy. Ethel said she wasn't surprised, she'd always had trouble from her men. She'd had to battle her way to keep on top. Gladys said nothing. She looked pretty put out and her face went scarlet when she heard. Effie hugged her, then she hugged Ethel. The three of them got a bit weepy until Dorothy began to push up against Effie, making her laugh. Lately Dorothy had started to break wind every five minutes, too. It stank to high heaven.

Effie was beginning to see Adin in a different light. He had come to live in this bach and he had fornicated with women, and was a dad many times over if what Pita said was the truth. Effie didn't know how the heck she could cope with it. It seemed to make a joke of their life together. Adin had not told her truth. 'Just as well it's in the past,' she told Gladys one night. 'It's all behind now, I'm certain. You and Ethel will have to pull your weight. I can't let it out to Lubin. It'd break his heart. He frets enough about what he did to the landlord.'

Effie told the girls everything. She fretted about Gladys and Ethel on the quiet. They didn't get on too good. They were from different backgrounds, different countries. Gladys didn't think much of Ethel, who had once given a load of money to Catholics. Ethel had quietly skited about that a few times. She'd helped out some nuns with money she'd made as a singer. Ethel reckoned Gladys was far too goody-goody and should have stayed in China, being a missionary.

'You've got to love each other,' Effie told them both. 'We're family now. We've all got to live together. Dorothy too when she's with us. Lubin won't like it if you're cranky with each other. He's the man of the house now, and I need you two.'

One afternoon, after they'd been sparking off at each other over something, Ethel had reckoned she might biff Gladys in the mouth. Ethel had started to tell Effie about her life, and Gladys kept butting in. Effie wondered if Gladys was jealous. Ethel had lived a pretty exciting life, having had a hard time of it when she was a little girl. Ethel had been a very poor black girl in Philadelphia, America. Ethel had been a bit naughty as a kiddy too, just as Effie had been. Effie reckoned they had a lot in common even though Ethel had become a famous jazz singer before she gave it all up to tour with Billy Good Man. She would have loved Adin to bits, Ethel told Effie.

She loved evangelists. Jesus, she told Effie, had been her playmate when she'd been a little tot. And Gladys kept spouting that she'd had a hard time of it too. She'd worked as a parlourmaid in England, had been slung off at for preaching to people in Hyde Park before she got away to China without a penny. Soon the two of them were yacking non-stop into Effie's ear. In the end Effie had to tell them both not to be so rowdy. She couldn't hear herself think, what with Dorothy galloping about all over the lino and falling over, as it was too slippery. That was when Ethel threatened to biff Gladys in the mouth.

'You're my friends and I love you,' Effie told the girls firmly. 'But you shouldn't squabble. You should be counting our blessings. Besides, I know all about you. I read your books ages ago.'

Lubin was away on Saul's land more and more. He still had a real crush on the animals. Effie fretted about that. The animals weren't his. She missed Lubin. Effie missed being on the road too. She put as much money away as she could out of what Saul paid Lubin for his jobs on the land. She had started to hanker after clearing out of Opononi, heading down south with Lubin, just as she and Adin had talked about clearing out to new pastures. She tried not to think about Adin back at Whangarei, lying like a cast-off piece of broken furniture. Up in Heaven Adin's soul would know she loved him. He'd know that Lubin still loved him. His body had been only his shell. Adin's soul was free. It would be beside the angels, with any luck.

'Can I come and live with yous, Missus Croft?' Pita asked her. He still came to see her every day. Effie still hadn't said a thing about Adin. She didn't know how. The other kiddies hadn't shown up for ages. 'My auntie wouldn't worry. I asked her. She's enough on her plate, she told me. I could be a orphan for you like Lubin is, I think.'

'Lubin isn't an orphan now, Pita, he's my son. He's nearly grown-up.'

'You don't need those funny ladies.' Pita told her. 'You could have me instead, ay. I'd be better than them ladies.'

Effie hugged him. They sat down at the table and tucked into fresh pikelets smothered in butter and jam. Pita asked if they could take Dorothy down to the beach to see the dolphin after eating the pikelets. 'Yous ladies have seen Opo. Dorothy hasn't,' he said. Effie reckoned that sounded like a good idea.

When they set off it was mid-afternoon. Effie wore her feather cloak, a flax sun-hat and jandals. They put Dorothy's halter on and then Effie polished her beak. Dorothy stood quite still while this was being done, but Pita got the giggles. When Effie asked him why, he pointed. As Effie polished Dorothy's beak, Dorothy was lifting up her right leg and shaking it.

There was a huge crowd outside the hotel. Some sort of party was going on, so they kept clear. Effie said to Pita that the blokes would all be boozing and were probably soaked with beer. 'My auntie, she boozes all the time,' Pita told her, grinning. 'She gets all soppy and giggles, but sometimes she cries and falls over.'

Effie held on to Pita with one hand, and on to Dorothy's lead with the other. She tried to ignore the stares. She reckoned the three of them might look a bit queer to some people. She held her head high. The sky above them was a deep, rich blue. The sun was scorching. The sand under their feet was hot. Effie could feel the heat through her jandals. Pita was barefoot and didn't seem to fret about the heat at all. He kept looking about and grinning at the staring faces. Most people grinned back. A few laughed. They were left alone at first.

Opo had been in the harbour for only a little while. There was a huge number of kiddies in the water. Effie spotted a few who had come to the bach, frolicking in the sea. People were packed like sardines along the jetty. Families were having picnics. Some bloke was organizing a sausage sizzle, and smoke rose up into the sky.

Opo was diving beneath several rowing-boats and small launches dotted about on the deep water. She was making her way slowly towards the shallows, where her favourite kiddies waited. Effie heard one bloke tell another that, a few days before, there'd been an accident. Opo had followed a fishing launch into the jetty. She had swum too close to the launch and been bashed on the head by the propellers, after which she had disappeared for a whole day. But she had come back as happy as Larry. The bloke said that Opo had leapt up out of the water to show people she was all right, despite the nasty cuts on her head. There had been blood in the water when it happened and everyone had been pretty shook about it. People loved Opo.

Effie and Pita watched as some bright spark chucked an empty beer bottle into the water near Opo as she swam inshore. Opo nosed it for a minute, then left it and dived. She came up with a different bottle, one she had found on the bottom. Effie cried out in wonder as Opo, balancing the bottle on her nose, threw it high into the air, repeating the performance when everyone cheered.

'She's a bit of a show-off, ay, Missus Croft,' said Pita.

'It's a fair miracle,' Effie said.

A cheer went up every time Opo made a leap out of the water. The sunlight shone brightly on her skin. Effie clapped her hands in glee. She jumped up and down, even though it made her legs a bit sore. Soon she and Pita were joined by the kiddies who had come to the bach. They all laughed and giggled. Some of the kiddies acted scared stiff of Dorothy. Dorothy stood on the sand shifting from one foot to the other. She stayed close beside Effie. Soon adults were coming up to ask questions. For a bit Effie became the centre of attraction. Dorothy had got a bit restless and was starting to yank on the halter and rear up against people. When she kicked someone on the leg, Effie whispered to Pita that they'd better get back and leave everyone to it.

'Don't yous want to get a paddle first?' Pita asked. 'We could paddle out and touch Opo like that other time. Dorothy'd like it, I think.'

But Effie just grinned and shook her head. Pita pouted.

Together they made their way back up to the road. None of the kiddies followed. The dolphin was the big attraction on the beach.

'The girls'll be frantic,' Effie said. 'They don't get on, Pita. Ethel wants to give Gladys a hiding, I'm certain. I can't risk more trouble.'

'Wish I could see them ladies, ay,' Pita muttered. He held on tight to Effie's hand as they headed across the marram grass towards the bach. Dorothy had calmed down now. She walked quietly along beside them. Effie saw the girl Lynette, who was Opo's favourite, according to Lubin. Lynette was standing staring. Effie gave her a huge smile and a wave. Lynette just stared back with her mouth wide open. Effie wondered if she was all there.

'I got to go home now, Missus Croft,' Pita suddenly blurted out before they'd reached the bach. 'My auntie, she'll be home and cooking.'

After saying hooray he ran off towards the hotel. He was soon gone from sight.

Effie felt a bit put out. She had planned to feed Pita herself. She knew he was a bit nervy of his auntie. 'Lubin'll be back soon, Dot,' she told Dorothy. 'He'll get you off home too, I suppose. Perhaps his boss will give you to us. That'd be good, ay? You could live with us in the bach. We'd have walks every day with the girls. We must count the blessings we've been given.'

Dorothy broke wind, then did a little leap.

Effie played the records on the gramophone. She sat at the window, staring out. She did this most days after Pita had gone and before Lubin turned up after his hard slog on the land. Lubin was always so worn out when he came home. Effie had gone back to sitting at the window in the rocking-chair. Dorothy stood beside her in the sunshine which streamed into the room. She preened her feathers. Effie rocked. They listened to the songs. Effie's legs ached quite a bit most days and she liked to sit quietly like this, the gramophone within reach of the chair so she could wind up the motor when it ran down. Through her memory slickered all the pictures of her life, all the moments she had been happy with Adin and Lubin on the road. She reckoned such happiness might not ever come again. When Lubin was not with her now she felt more lonely than she had ever felt before. She sat and rocked in silence when she played the records. Dorothy crouched on the lino, falling asleep in the late afternoon sun. It was still scorching.

The day slowly waned, the light fading, and then Lubin came home for his tea. Effie cooked mince on toast and made two banana surprises for pudding.

Lubin was quieter than usual after he had returned from taking Dorothy back to Saul's farm. He was filthy dirty. He had cobwebs clinging to his shorts. He was drenched with sweat and looked a little shook.

'Have a bath, son, there's gallons of hot water,' Effie said.

Lubin gave her a weak grin. He was acting a bit shifty and wouldn't look her in the eye. When he went off to the bathroom, Effie thought about what Pita had told her. She had managed to shove it aside for days. Now she wondered if Lubin somehow knew as well, the way he was acting. Trying to keep it from her so she'd have no worries. Lubin might have talked to Pita. Pita might have asked Lubin if he knew his Mr Adin. She'd like to keep the truth from Lubin. But how the heck could she? It would cause a rift if she did. It might pull them apart. Effie felt a bit jittery and covered her face with her hands.

Outside, the dark had fallen. The air had become chilly. Effie could hear Lubin in the bath. After his splashing stopped, he sang in his clear and beaut voice. He sang Ethel Waters's song, 'His Eye Is on the Sparrow'. He knew all the words off by heart. As they came through to where Effie sat, she reckoned she had no choice but to tell Lubin about Pita's bombshell. She couldn't keep tight about it, she had to share it with him. For she and Lubin had faced everything together and needed one another like heck.

They were drinking Milo at the kitchen table hours later when they both heard the noise out back. Effie had been trying to get up the gall to tell Lubin about Pita's bombshell. While Lubin had been trying to find a way of telling Effie his bit of news, so that she wouldn't get too frantic. About what he had found on Saul's land. Instead they had talked about everything else. It was dead quiet, for by now it was quite late. They had been speaking in near-whispers. The noise out back came so clearly, they both froze. It was a loud cracking of twigs.

Effie whispered, 'There's somebody out there.'

Lubin put a finger to his lips. They stayed still, listening. The sound of cracking twigs came again. Somebody was out back, moving through the bush.

'It might just be a stray dog, Mum,' Lubin whispered

back. But his face gave him away. He was scared stiff.

'It could be Pita. You'd better have a look,' Effie told him.

Lubin fetched the torch from the kitchen cupboard. With Effie right behind him he opened the back door and peered out.

'I'm glad the girls are fast asleep. They'd have made a racket, I'm certain,' Effie whispered.

Lubin motioned for her to say nothing more. They stepped down into the yard. Lubin shone the torch towards the bush. There was a sudden flurry of movement and noise, then silence. They looked at each other, Effie hanging on to Lubin's arm. The noise had come from close to where the landlord lay buried. The night was as dark as pitch. The moon was hidden behind cloud. There weren't any stars. Lubin swung the torch beam slowly across the area where the bush began. There was no one there. There was no movement now. Sounds of voices came from the motor camp, like a gentle buzzing that didn't stop. Effie began shivering, for it was pretty chilly. Frost was forming on the grass.

'You get back in,' Lubin told her quietly. 'I'll have a look. It might just be some dog.'

'You be careful, son,' Effie said. She didn't go inside but stood on the bach steps watching as Lubin crossed the yard.

Lubin stepped into the bush, moving out of sight. Then it grew quiet. Effie couldn't even see the beam of the torch. She almost shrieked when suddenly she saw a shape hurtling across the grass. It was a possum. The possum stopped for a minute and made a squeaking noise before it ran off towards the far side of the yard and went out of sight. Effie had never seen a possum move so fast. She was about to go after Lubin, as he hadn't come back, when there came the noise of an engine starting up close by. It didn't sound like a car, more like a motor bike. There were a heck of a lot of bikes around the settlement. Just as it revved up, Effie got the beam of the torch right in her eyes and she yelled out. But it was only Lubin. He hurried over to her and they went inside. Lubin bolted the door.

Effie put on the jug and started to make some more Milo. 'Who was it, son, who was it?' she asked, turning to look at Lubin.

He shrugged. 'I couldn't see anyone.' he said.

'Has someone been near the grave?' Effie whispered.

Lubin shook his head.

'I reckon they must've gone by now,' Effie carried on. 'It could've been a burglar. There's a load of queer people around, I heard somebody say on the beach. I thought the girls'd wake up. I made such a racket when you shone the torch in my face. I saw a possum!'

Lubin sat down at the table, staring at the torch in his hands.

When the Milo was ready, Effie brought a jugful and sat beside him. 'It's all right,' she said. 'Don't get het up. Nothing happened, ay? It was probably some drunken lout, the place is full up with all sorts. They're bound to nose about. They say people from the city stay up all night carousing. We scared him off, whoever it was.' Effie poured out the Milo into mugs. 'Drink up, son, it'll do you good. I've got something to tell you. It isn't the right time, but I've got to get it off my chest. You've got to know. I don't want Pita letting it out.'

Lubin looked up then and stared at her.

After a few minutes Effie told him. 'It's a bit of a sticky piece of news,' she finished off. 'It's been a shock, son. I haven't slept for nights. I didn't think it could be true at first, but I reckon it must be. Pita's a good boy.'

'You don't think Pita might be fibbing?' Lubin asked when she had stopped. While she had been talking to him Lubin had reached over and held her hand real tight.

'No, Lubin, how could he? He wouldn't tell fibs to me, I'm certain. I haven't let on about anything. But I reckon he's telling the truth. Your dad's been a dark horse. He came here when he pushed off all those times.'

'The bastard,' Lubin said loudly. 'The rotten bastard.'

'No, Lubin, son, don't say that about your dad!' Effie cried out.

Lubin got up, pushing back his chair. Effie struggled to her feet and reached out to him. But Lubin was gone, and he slammed the door behind him.

Effie sat down again at the table. She covered her face with her hands. She held them there for a long time. After a while she heard Lubin bawling his eyes out.

Lubin didn't go off to Saul's farm the next morning. 'I can't face that place today, Mum,' he told Effie. 'I'd like to stay with you.'

They were standing at the oven. Lubin put his arms round Effie and hugged her. Effie hugged him back.

'It'll be all right, son,' Effie said quietly when Lubin pulled away. 'It's in the past, ay? The Evangelist will have had to answer to his Maker. We've got to grin and bear it.'

'What about what we've done – what about that?' Lubin said. 'It's all wrong!'

Effie looked at Lubin and got a shock. For suddenly he looked like a grown-up. He wasn't a little boy any longer, with a grin enough to open Heaven's Gate. He was a young man with a will of his own. He looked like somebody she didn't know and it frightened her a bit, the way he had spoken.

Later that morning Pita showed up. He grinned from ear to ear seeing Lubin still at the bach. Lubin took him out into the front yard. He and Pita sat under a kowhai tree to talk. Effie watched from the window. The two of them stayed there talking for a long time. Effie went back to the kitchen, where Gladys and Ethel were sitting at the table. The girls looked as worried as Effie felt.

When Lubin came back indoors he was on his own. Pita had pushed off to the beach. Lubin had told him to come back the next day to see Effie. 'I explained who his Mr Adin was,' Lubin said. 'It was Dad, no mistake.'

'What did Pita say?' Effie asked.

Lubin gave her a long look. 'He didn't catch on for a while. Then he started crying. He said he'd always wanted a big brother. Said you could be his mum if you wanted, any day.'

Effie was choked up. She turned away and covered her face.

After lunch Lubin went out the back on his own for quite a while. Effie reckoned he was in the bush, checking the grave. He fretted over it all the time. Effie had been showing Ethel how to do crocheting, just to keep herself busy. Ethel had told her she'd never had the time to crochet. When Lubin came in, Effie was laughing like billy-o at something Ethel had said. The girls had got into a tangle with the cotton. Lubin sat down at the table. He stared at Effie.

Effie stopped laughing. 'What's the matter, son – you're not crook, are you?' she asked.

Lubin shook his head. He carried on looking into Effie's face. Then he blurted out. 'I found the landlord's green motor bike out on the farm yesterday, Mum. It was hidden in one of Saul's sheds. It was hidden under canvas. The landlord came up here on it that day. I saw it down the road. I looked for it after, but it'd gone.'

'Saul Smith must've pinched it, then,' said Effie. 'It'd be worth a few bob, I'm certain.'

Lubin still acted shifty. He got up from his chair. Then he sat down again. He stared at Effie as if he didn't see her. Effie looked a bit puzzled.

96

'I reckon Saul Smith's not who we think he is,' Lubin said.

Effie didn't answer. She could see that Lubin was shook. She didn't get why. After a while she got up and reckoned she'd cook some pikelets.

Lubin sat staring at her.

9   A Bit of Strife

'You've got to forgive your dad,' Effie told Lubin a few days later. 'I've done it in my heart, I'm certain.' She was feeling a bit windy, waiting for Pita to show up. Lubin had told her twice he blamed Adin for everything that had gone on since he had died.

Effie didn't sleep well at night. She kept getting out of bed and peering through the windows thinking she had heard a noise. They should never have come to this place, Lubin kept telling her. They should have guessed it would cause trouble. He was still fretting about finding the landlord's motor bike out on the farm. He reckoned it did mean something. He fretted, while Effie's cooking kept her mind off things. She had baked some fly cemeteries. 'You should have a try at baking cakes,' Effie told him. 'Cooking helps. You could use my "Aunt Daisy" cookbook, it's easy.'

They were sitting at the table in the kitchen. The cakes were piled high on a plate. Lubin hadn't touched them. Effie had offered the plate to Ethel and Gladys, but they weren't too keen either. Gladys didn't like the look of fly cemeteries.

After a silence Lubin said, 'He must've got the TB off her.'

Effie stared at him blankly.

'Dad,' said Lubin. 'Pita's mum must've given it to him. Pita said his mum was pretty crook with the TB for a long time. Then she got well and shoved off to Sydney. She'd been getting proper treatment.'

'No, son, the timing couldn't be right,' Effie said quickly. 'We should do something for little Pita. I wonder where he's got to. He hasn't anybody except that auntie. He's your half-brother, Lubin.'

Lubin hadn't gone back to the farm. Saul hadn't showed up to find out where he was.

'I'm not going back there to work, Mum,' Lubin told Effie. 'I reckon something fishy's going on. Why would he take that bike and hide it?'

'I don't know, son. It probably doesn't mean anything. That man's a queer sort, though. Ethel noticed things about him that time he came here to tell us who he was. Ethel's a sharp sort. She said she wouldn't trust him. Ethel reckoned the way he dumped those presents on us and then showed up should've made us get the wind-up. It wasn't normal for a bloke to act like that.'

It was warm in the kitchen. The sunlight was streaming through the windows. There was hardly a breath of air outside. People were still surging into the settlement from all over the country and now from overseas. Opo the dolphin was a giant attraction. She was being worshipped. Some bloke had written a song about her. Lubin said he'd heard that Opononi would never be the same place again, according to the locals.

The new year was well on the way. It was nearly March. Even Effie thought about winter up ahead and how they would get themselves warm when it showed up. There was no heater in the bach except the oven. Ethel had pointed out to Effie that winter here was codswallop compared with where she came from. Snow fell there. Sometimes people died. In New Zealand people were spoilt by the good weather. Ethel had some pretty odd notions at times, Effie had noticed. Yet she loved and cherished both her and Gladys. The girls gave her comfort, just by being near.

'Why did Dad keep on coming up here like that? What

99

was he really after?' Lubin asked. 'He always kept so tight about it.'

Effie felt her face get hot. She reached across the table and held on tight to Lubin's hands. 'I didn't know then either, son,' she said. 'It's clear now. I reckon it was my dicky womb. You remember, I told you about that. Your dad didn't want to touch me after we found out.' Effie hung her head. 'He wanted kiddies like I did,' she added.

'Didn't Dad love you?' Lubin asked.

'We always loved each other, Lubin! Your dad, he had big needs, he was a bloke who had big needs of the flesh. He must've come up here all those times he went off because he found what he was after. He kept coming back for more. He'd have been too ashamed to let on to me.' Effie drew Lubin's hands up to her and kissed them. 'His flesh was weak, son. Most men have weakness of the flesh.'

''Struth, no wonder he wanted to die,' Lubin said. 'He must have been real ashamed. He must've been coming up here for a heck of a long time, Mum. Pita's nearly nine!'

'Lubin – don't, son, please,' said Effie. Lubin got up from his chair and knelt down on the floor beside her. 'You've got to love him always,' Effie said. 'He always loved me. He loved you. You and I'll never understand any of it, so there's no use trying. It's in the past now.'

After a while a little squinting face appeared at the window. The face peered in at them, staring at what was on the table. Then a voice called out, 'Missus Croft, Missus Croft, can I come in and eat a cake? Fly cemeteries is my favourites, ay.'

It was Pita.

Pita ate four fly cemeteries before he asked Effie if he'd be allowed to see her ladies now. 'Yous relations now, ay, Missus Croft,' Pita said. He looked pretty shy and hung his head. 'I think yous could be my mum and my brother. Them ladies, they could be my aunties, I reckon. I can't see them when I look, though.'

Effie wiped her eyes. She grinned and gave Pita a hug. With Pita there the tension had eased off a bit. Effie felt a bit put out, but she introduced Ethel and Gladys to Pita formally. She told the girls who Pita really was. Then she told Pita all about the girls, though he had heard it all before. Lubin sat looking on, grinning.

When Effie stopped talking, Pita stared round the room, squinting. After a long time his face brightened. 'I sees them!' he sang out. 'Boy, they look a bit nifty, ay. I'd like them to be my aunties, I think. They could take me along the shops and buy me lollies.'

After Effie had gone off to wash her face, Pita looked shyly at Lubin. 'You still work for that Saul Griff bugger?' he whispered.

Lubin went to answer. But when what Pita had said sunk in, his face became pale. 'Saul Griff?' he asked.

'Yeah, the animal man. You feed his animals, ay? Boy, that's a stinky job, I bet. I wouldn't do it.'

'You mean Saul Smith,' said Lubin.

'That's not his name. It's Saul Griff. Dunno why you work for him. Everyone's scared of that joker. He's a real bugger. He and his brother was in the hotel one night and they tried to shove a knife in another bloke for somethink. My auntie says Saul Griff has so much booze in him all the time, he pisses beer. He knocked her over once and she told him to frig off, and he did. He wasn't worried. He keeps coming back.'

Lubin stayed silent. In his stare Pita shifted about in his seat. 'He tried to root my mum once,' Pita whispered. Then he giggled, his hands across his mouth.

Lubin got up from the table pretty quick, nearly knocking it over. He left Pita alone and shut himself into the bathroom with Effie.

Pita stared about the room before he ate another cake.

When Lubin and Effie came back Effie's face was a deep red. 'You must of scrubbed your face too hard,' said Pita, grinning at Effie.

Lubin and Effie sat down at the table beside Pita. While Lubin asked Pita questions, Effie sat wringing her hands.

Saul was the Whangarei landlord's brother. Pita remembered the brother because both of them had taken his mum out for nights at the hotel. 'It was ages before she met Mr Adin, but she told me all about thems,' Pita said. 'They was both still around when I was born, I think. But after I got born, Mum got all good and read the Bible for a while until she got crook. Mum was a bit proud of Mr Adin. My auntie says those Griffs took my mum out lots a times. They only wanted to put their dongs in her.'

Effie was shocked. She stared at Pita then asked him how he could know about such things.

'Oh, I'se had lotsa uncles when Mum was around. They were all after her. My mum was real beaut looking. My auntie, she knows all about it. You should ask her. Saul Griff still comes over some nights, but he just gets drunk and scratches his bum a lot.'

Pita could not know what all this meant to Effie and Lubin, Effie reckoned, though he could easily find out. He knew so much. She changed the subject. Pita chatted away at them now without stopping. He had so much to say bottled up inside him about his life that it poured out. Pita trembled, from being allowed to talk for so long.

The Griff brothers, according to Pita, were well known. Everyone in the settlement knew about them. Saul and his brother had had a big fight in the hotel one night over his mum, Pita told them. After that the brother pushed off to live somewhere else. They were nasty blokes and could get real rough and both had bad tempers. Pita couldn't figure out why Effie and Lubin liked Saul Griff.

Effie couldn't credit how much Pita seemed to know. He was a tiny tyke with an old head. She reckoned he must be a lonely boy, his mum having shoved off and as he'd lost a dad without really having had one to start off with.

'Nobody likes that pakeha because he explodes the fishes,' Pita told them. 'Auntie reckons he's always up to no good.'

Effie spent the rest of the day fretting. She fretted about Dorothy, which took her mind off the latest bombshell from Pita. Now she knew who Saul really was, it choked her that Dorothy was stuck out there on the farm with that bloke who wasn't a Smith but a Griff, and a nasty sort like his brother had been. He could be even worse. He could find out about the grave. There was no question of Lubin's going back to the farm to carry on working. Effie reckoned he wouldn't cope with any more friction, it was getting too dangerous.

Lubin was only too pleased to take Pita off down to the harbour. They were going to dig for shellfish under the jetty. Effie stayed inside the bach. She locked the doors and pulled down the blinds. She was scared stiff that Saul Griff might show up at any time.

Lubin and Pita came back without any shellfish. They both looked a bit sheepish. Effie asked them what they'd been up to.

'We went out to the farm,' Lubin told her. 'It's all right, he wasn't there. Everything's locked up. We didn't go close, we hid. He's done a bunk, by the look of it.'

'What about Dorothy?' Effie asked.

'She was in her pen, she's all right. There was a lot of

food on the ground.'

'I reckon we should give the cloak and the gramophone back, Lubin,' Effie said. 'We can't keep them, not now we know who that man is. I've been thinking, I'm worn out from thinking. It wouldn't be right if we kept them. I don't get why he gave them to us.'

'Yous could hide them at my house,' Pita said. 'My auntie she wouldn't know. She's got a new bloke she's being all soppy over. She does it behind my back, but I seen her through the window. She wouldn't notice.'

Lubin didn't say a thing. He stared at Pita. Effie made a pot of tea. Pita ate another fly cemetery. Then he sat, looking queasy. After a while he grinned at them and turned his head, staring across the room. 'I'se eating all the fly cemeteries up, Auntie Ethel!' he sang out, and giggled, looking at Effie. Effie hugged him.

While the tea was drawing in the pot, Lubin said to Effie, 'I'm going back out there after dark. I'll get Dorothy and bring her back here. She can stay with us. I'll have a scout around and see what's up. It looked like he might've been gone for ages. He could've just dumped Dorothy.'

They sat and talked about Lubin's making a night raid to rescue the emu. Effie worried that it would just bring on more trouble, but Lubin shrugged. Pita wanted to go on the raid too, but Lubin wasn't too keen on that. 'You should be getting off home, Pita,' he told him. 'What about your auntie – doesn't she worry?'

'Nah, she'll be right. She'll be up at the hotel with her new bloke. He's a shearer from Mangamuka. He's a pakeha like Mr Adin. He gave me five shillings and said not to worry him and Auntie.'

'You'll have to get home straight after,' Effie told Pita.

'Can we take the aunties? Auntie Ethel – she'd like to have a raid, I think,' Pita said, grinning.

Effie just shook her head. 'You can watch out for

Lubin, Pita,' she said. 'But I want you to be real careful, ay? You do everything Lubin tells you.'

'All right, I will,' said Pita.

They set off after it was dark. Lubin wore his Balaclava and dark clothes. Effie gave Pita her sun-glasses to wear. He had wanted a better disguise. 'I like dressing up,' he said. He'd asked to wear the feather cloak and one of her hats, but Effie said no.

Before opening the door Effie switched off the light. There was no moon and it was very dark. Pita was shivering. 'Onward, soldiers,' Effie said as they went down into the yard. They could hear a bit of revelry coming from outside the hotel, but the night was mostly quiet. It was cold. Already dew was forming. It was only a little past ten o'clock. Effie had made Pita have a sleep on her bed after tea. He had grizzled when she had woken him up just before ten. Effie had given them a blanket to put over Dorothy. She told them not to forget Dorothy's halter. 'Good luck!' she whispered as they careered off out into the dark.

'Tata, Missus Croft!' Pita yelled out. 'We'll be good!'

Effie heard Lubin telling him to shut up and be quiet as she hurried back inside.

Lubin and Pita ran all the way to the edge of Saul's land. They kept away from the hotel and the other buildings. They ran low through bush so no one would spot them. There wasn't anybody about. The hotel had closed now and most people had gone straight home or back to the motor camp because of the cold night. Pita folded the blanket round him. He told Lubin that he felt like Hone Heke, the Maori warrior. 'It would've been even better with that cloak,' he said. 'More real, ay, Lubin? Maori warriors always wore cloaks.'

'You know a lot, ay, Pita?' Lubin said as they crouched

105

down behind flax, getting their wind back.

'When yous with me you could talk like a Maori too if you like,' Pita said. 'I could teach you. Maoris are better than pakehas. We're not all crooks like yous pakeha buggers. And we're bloody stronger. You don't get no sissy Maoris.'

Lubin told him he shouldn't swear. 'Effie doesn't like swearing, Pita. You might swear in front of her. You'll have to watch it.'

'Oh, all right,' said Pita. 'But I wouldn't swear in front of a lady anyway. I'll only swear when you're bloody round, ay, Lubin.'

When they'd got their breath back Lubin peered over the top of the flax. 'I don't think Saul's around. Come on, you follow me and stay close. And be quiet.'

They ran across the shallow stream that was the back boundary of the farm. Lubin had brought a torch, but there was light enough to see from the moon and stars. They could hear mopokes calling. Both of them nearly yelled out loud when a branch from a ponga cracked off and fell near where they stood still, watching the farmhouse. There were no lights on inside at all. None showed from any of the sheds. The place looked deserted. Lubin whispered to Pita that he wanted to have a look around before they got Dorothy out from her pen. They could both see her. She was standing in the far corner of her pen, facing them. She didn't make a sound.

'She knows we're here,' Pita whispered. 'She's not dumb, ay?'

Lubin, with Pita right behind him, raced across the bare earth, past a group of cabbage trees to the shed where Lubin had discovered the motor bike. The doors squeaked loudly as they pulled them open. They stayed still for a full minute listening, but there was no response to the noise. Lubin felt certain that Saul Griff wasn't anywhere on the farm. The motor bike wasn't in the shed.

'He's pushed off, I bet,' Lubin whispered. 'He could show up any time, Pita, so we'd better be quick.'

Lubin made Pita stay in the yard while he checked the other buildings. The fur seals, pelicans and the rabbits were all gone. The cages of the rare birds, the kiwis and keas, were empty. The guinea pigs weren't to be seen. The goats had been set free into the paddock behind the farmhouse. In the distance Lubin could make out their shapes in the faint starlight. They were standing and sitting amongst bushes. Lubin reckoned the goats knew he was there. They didn't miss much. Lubin couldn't figure out why Saul had taken away all the animals, or how he had managed it. He reckoned it meant something. It confused him too, because Dorothy had been left behind. Lubin wondered if Saul might even be now on his way back from somewhere, to get Dorothy.

When Lubin got back, Pita had fallen fast asleep in the yard against one of the fence-posts. The blanket was still wrapped round him. Lubin almost fell over him. Pita yelled out and grizzled when Lubin woke him up.

The two of them hurried across the yard to the pen and pulled open the rickety gate. On the gate hung Dorothy's halter. They put it on Dorothy as quickly as they could and tried to cover her with the blanket. Dorothy jumped into the air each time the blanket settled across her back. It kept sliding off. After a few tries Pita wrapped the blanket round himself again. He was shivering with cold. His teeth chattered. Lubin told him to jump up and down on the spot to get warm. As he did so, Dorothy made a few leaps and pushed herself against Lubin.

Lubin suddenly froze, reaching out to grab Pita's arm. They heard the sound of the motor at the same time, far off and faint, coming towards the farmhouse from the south. Lubin's mouth went dry. He was certain the sound was the motor bike and that Saul would be on it.

'The bugger's coming back!' Pita yelled out, seeing Lubin's face.

Lubin, in a panic, clapped his hands over Pita's mouth.

10   Dorothy Gets Saved

Effie sat in her rocking-chair, in the dark. She had got scared once the boys had gone. She reckoned if anyone saw lights they might knock on the door, it was so late. She kept thinking she could hear footsteps on the gravel path out front. She didn't have a look in case there really was someone prowling. Now the hotel had shut for the night she could hear breakers on the beach, but little else. Her heart was thudding. She took deep breaths and wished Ethel and Gladys hadn't gone off to bed the way they had, leaving her in the lurch. She could have done with their company, though they might have made a bit of noise and wanted the lights on.

'Are you girls still awake?' Effie whispered into the quiet. She heard no response. After a while she got up out of the chair and tiptoed to one of the windows. There was a crack in the blind. She put her face close and peered through. She couldn't see anything, just darkness. Holding her breath she pulled the blind an inch away from the frame. She looked out.

Effie shrieked and jumped back into the room. She almost fell over. The holland blind had suddenly come away from its catch. The blind rolled up, flapping loudly. Coming out of its socket it fell down over her head. Unravelled, the blind blocked her sight. As she struggled to yank it off, she was certain there was someone on the other side of the window, looking in. Shouting 'Go away, go away!' she pulled the blind free. She let it fall, her eyes shut tight. For a moment she couldn't move. When she opened her eyes and looked, there was no one out in the yard. There was nobody along the road. The light from the stars and the moon made everything seem so bright. She stood shaking, staring towards the sand-hills across the harbour. Nothing moved. Effie covered her face with her hands. She took a few deep breaths before fixing the blind, hoping that the boys, and Dorothy, would hurry up and come back.

The sound of the motor out on the farmhouse road came closer. It got louder and louder. Lubin had yanked Pita down, knocking Dorothy off balance. Lubin lay on top of Pita squashed between Dorothy and the fence. Unable to stay there, he slowly hauled himself up. He peered towards the road across Dorothy's back. He whispered to Pita not to move. A van was coming along the road. It wasn't the motor bike after all. The van sped past without slowing down. It was gone in less than a minute. Lubin watched the tail lights until they disappeared from sight. Dorothy hadn't shifted, apart from shuffling her feet from side to side, managing to stand on Lubin's feet and on Pita's hands. She was stretching up and peering at them with a real snooty look.

'Boy,' said Pita, clambering to his feet, 'that was bloody close, ay, Lubin! What'll we do now?'

'We'll be right,' Lubin said, laughing, his face red.

They both grinned with relief. Lubin felt like a bit of a drip. He should have known it wasn't a motor bike they had heard. The sound was too different. Lubin gave Pita a quick hug.

Dorothy came quietly out of the pen with them. She stood close to Lubin's side, twitching her feathers. Pita reckoned she looked as though she was in a paddy. She was put out at being knocked.

'I'll have to come back for some feed,' Lubin told Pita.

'There's some in the shed, I think. He's just left Dorothy, I reckon. He's dumped her. You hang on here, there's something I want to check again first. Hold on to Dorothy for me.'

Lubin crept around the outside of the house, peering in through the windows, trying to open each one. The front door was locked. The back door was locked. He tried to force both of them, but they wouldn't budge. In the yard, Dorothy broke wind. The sound was so loud, Pita got the giggles. He let go of the halter lead, and then Dorothy was off like a rocket, running towards Lubin. Now she began tearing round and round in circles, leaping up every few steps and careering about. Lubin and Pita had to chase after her. Dorothy thought it was a game. She ran faster. They were so stonkered by the time Lubin managed to catch her that it was slow going when they set out, back the way they had come. They were pretty winded. Just as it had happened before, Dorothy refused to cross the stream once she had stepped into it. She stood shaking each of her feet and wouldn't go forward. In the end, after a lot of coaxing, which made no difference, Lubin had to pick her up and carry her. Dorothy acted as if she liked being carried. In Lubin's arms she twisted her head back and rubbed it against his face. Then she pecked at his hair. Once they had crossed the stream Dorothy walked close beside Pita. Lubin had given him the halter lead. Dorothy shoved herself sideways against Pita every few yards, trying to knock him off balance. She kept breaking wind, then making little jumps. Pita got helpless with giggles. Lubin took the lead back.

It was now well after midnight. Lubin didn't have a watch, but it seemed as though they had left Effie for far too long. A cold dew was falling. It dampened their clothes. The breakers along the shore sounded closer than they were. Overhead they heard a night plane passing.

111

The falling dew stopped them from seeing it when they looked up. Somewhere close by as they neared the hotel a couple of cats were having a fight. They were making a real racket.

Effie was hiding under the kitchen table clutching a broom when they reached the bach. She had heard them coming and reckoned it was Saul Griff. When she realized it was her boys she crawled out, laughing a bit. She hugged them, looking sheepish. Lubin told her about the rescue. Pita kept interrupting. 'We were real brave like Maori blokes, ay,' he kept saying. From the moment she saw Effie, Dorothy wouldn't leave her alone. She followed Effie about, pecking gently at the top of Effie's head and pushing up against her.

'She's missed you a bit, Mum,' Lubin said.

When Effie went out of the kitchen, Dorothy followed close behind, rearing up against Effie's back, her neck and head held above Effie.

'Bags I stay the night?' Pita asked Effie when she came back. 'No one'll miss me. Auntie'll be too boozed up, I think.'

'No, Lubin will take you home, Pita. That's best, I'm certain.'

Pita's face puckered, but then he tried to look brave. 'Oh, all right. I can get through my window, I think. I left it open. Can I come back tomorrow? I like being here, Missus Croft. You could be my real mum if you like.'

Effie became still. She had her back to Pita. She was standing in front of the oven warming the teapot. For a moment Effie put her hands up and covered her face. Then she turned round and pulled Pita to her. She held his face tightly against her without saying anything. After a minute Lubin took Pita by the arm and led him across the kitchen and out the back door. Effie stood there, her face twisted. Lubin hadn't wanted Pita to see it. Pita's eyes were almost shut. He was half asleep, conked out

112

from having been on the randan with Lubin.

By the time Lubin got back, having helped Pita climb through the window at his auntie's house, Effie had made up a bed for Dorothy on the kitchen floor. She had laid down newspaper and blankets. Dorothy was crouched on the bed. She was busy digging into feathers with her beak. Effie had put on her nightie and dressing-gown. She was pale with tiredness, just as Lubin was. They hugged for a long time. Effie's head rested on Lubin's shoulder. Lubin stroked her hair. After the hug they went to bed.

Lubin didn't sleep much. He was up again before dawn. He got dressed quietly and slipped out of the bach without waking Effie. He shut the kitchen door and left by the front so Dorothy wouldn't hear him and make a racket. Before the sky had begun to get light he ran along the road and down the side of the hotel. He made his way towards the farmhouse, scared stiff he'd see Saul Griff there.

The farm was still deserted. Lubin searched the sheds and found some small bags of mixed grain. Fretting he'd get caught, he left as quickly as he could. The bags were heavy, yet he lugged them and ran part of the way back to Èffie and Dorothy. Nothing happened. No one shouted out. He was back in the kitchen before Effie woke up.

Effie hid the bags of grain behind the dunny, under an old tarpaulin. They saw no sign of Pita that day. He didn't show up. Lubin didn't spot him about the settlement when he went down to the beach to mix with the crowds. Effie kept Dorothy inside the bach. She planned to let her out into the yard only after dark. Dorothy kept breaking wind and pooping all over the kitchen lino. Effie spent most of the day clearing up the muck. It stank the bach out. She fed Dorothy on the grain and cut up raw vegies. There weren't many vegies left in the safe by the end of the day.

Effie told Lubin that even the girls were feeling friction. Ethel had reckoned to her earlier that they should clear out now while the going was good and before any coppers showed up to haul them off to gaol. They could get the jalopy cranked up somehow. They could all go. Saul Griff was certain to show up now, after Dorothy. He'd find out about the dead and buried landlord and then where would they be? Men were always trouble, Ethel told Effie. Ethel had ticked off Gladys, who kept going on about their all being up to no good here. Gladys didn't like it one bit, it wasn't Christian.

'I'm worrying about Pita, son,' Effie told Lubin. 'Where's he got to? That's what we want to know. Gladys is getting het up. She's certain the little tyke's been taken off. He might have got taken off by you know who. Pita said he'd be back today.'

'Do you want me to have another scout around?' Lubin asked.

'Only if you're careful, son. Pita might be in trouble. That man knows he comes here. He must have known who Pita's real dad is all along. And he's certain to cause trouble over us pinching Dorothy.'

Lubin had checked the landlord's grave a few times. He said nothing to Effie. She'd put the grave out of her mind, he reckoned. Effie seemed to find it hard saying Saul's name aloud now.

That night once it had got dark they sat together, with Dorothy, in the kitchen. They expected Saul to show up at any time. Effie kept the oven switched on for warmth and left the oven door open. Dorothy had begun to sit in front of the oven on one of the blankets. She stuck her head inside the oven. Effie reckoned it was just as well they didn't have gas like people did in the Old Country. Yet Effie acted scared. She was nervy. She jumped at the smallest sounds. Lubin felt the same way but didn't let on. He took off to Pita's auntie's house after it had been dark a few hours. He was gone only a short time. Effie waited, sitting quietly. She wished they had a radio. The place was too quiet, yet she needed to keep listening.

When Lubin got back he said to Effie, 'The place looks empty, there's no sign of anyone. There's a car parked in the drive, but it doesn't have any wheels.'

'They must be there, they wouldn't leave a car,' Effie said.

'I'll have another look tomorrow,' Lubin said.

Effie was sitting with Dorothy in front of her. Dorothy's top half rested on Effie's lap. Her neck was balanced across Effie's shoulder. Effie carried on stroking Dorothy's head and scratching her back.

The next morning Lubin searched the beach. There were less people about, as the weather was chilly. Opo was still appearing every day, to perform for the more gentle visitors and have her photograph taken. People were filming her with modern cine-cameras. Lubin felt a bit too worried to enjoy watching. He went back to where Pita lived. He saw no one there. It worried him all the more, but he said little to Effie. He stayed close to her and Dorothy after his search. They talked about what they should do, that it might be better if they did just pack up and clear out. Get back on the road. Effie reckoned they could shoot down to Wellington, get on the Picton ferry and head south. They'd take Pita if they could find him. Try to give him a good life and try to be good from now on themselves. Keep away from authorities and trouble. 'That's what the Evangelist would've wanted, son,' Effie said. 'But you're doing all right being in charge. It's a hard life.'

Effie got frantic the following morning when Lubin told

her that it looked like Saul Griff might be back. Lubin had been out to the farmhouse and seen a lorry parked outside. He hadn't seen Saul.

'It could've been someone else,' Effie said. But after a bit she started to wring her hands. They stayed together quietly all day. Lubin kept watch from the windows. Effie fretted even more when she found out that there was no food left for them and only a little for Dorothy. Dorothy had eaten most of hers and all of theirs. She ate like a horse, not an emu, Effie told Lubin. But she was too scared to let Lubin go along to the shops.

'Let's wait a bit, he might spot you. He'll be watching out, I'm certain. He'll be setting the coppers on to us for pinching Dorothy. He'll have figured where she is. I reckon he knows more about us than he's let on. What if he suspects something, what if he finds the grave, ay?'

Effie went on and on all day like that. Lubin felt like clearing off down to the beach but didn't dare leave her alone.

Late that night Effie was in the front room making certain all the windows were shut. She looked out and thought she saw a figure standing behind a Norfolk pine on the far side of the road, beyond the empty section next door. The figure was watching the bach. Effie's heart thumped. She couldn't get her breath for a minute. When she was certain that it was Saul Griff lurking there, she drew back. She couldn't make out the figure very clearly except for the face. In the light from the moon the face looked like the face of the Devil.

After that she crawled into bed with Lubin, but she kept tight about seeing the figure. She lay there wide awake beside him as he slept, listening. There were no sounds from outside. Effie lay holding Lubin to her, waiting for the dawn to come.

By the morning a heavy rain was falling. When Effie got up and looked out, all she could see was a greyness.

116

There was no one about. She made breakfast by boiling some of the rice she found at the back of the safe. She fed some of the grain to Dorothy. When Lubin came out they sat in the kitchen without much energy for talk. Lubin told her he'd get along to the shops some time in the day to buy food. He'd have to go. Effie rummaged about for money before they made up a list. 'We'll need lots of rice,' she said. 'Dorothy can eat that.'

'If she's still here,' Lubin muttered.

Effie just stared at him but didn't reply.

Effie had a sleep in her own bed after breakfast. Lubin let Dorothy out into the back yard. The rain was still falling. Dorothy took a few steps across the sodden grass, then came back inside. She stood shaking her feet. Then she shook her whole body, showering Lubin with water, and walked across to the oven, shoving her head inside it. She pecked at something. The kitchen floor had got covered with poop during the night. Lubin cleaned up the muck and washed down the lino. Dorothy was trying to push herself into the oven. Then she backed out and slipped on the wet floor, knocking over the scrub bucket. Suds and hot water poured everywhere. Lubin was certain the noise would wake Effie. He quietened Dorothy after mopping up the water. He stroked her head and neck until her eyes closed and she swayed from side to side as if she were drunk. 'You're a real loony,' Lubin said.

While Effie slept on, Lubin tore down to the Four Square to get as much groceries and rice as they could afford. The couple who ran the grocer's treated him as they always did. They asked after Effie. They talked non-stop. They kept interrupting each other as they always did, laughing like billy-o. Everything seemed normal. They'd wondered where Lubin had got to. The wife, Ailene, gave Lubin for free a cooked mutton-bird and some fresh scones that had been left over from a party at the hotel. The husband, whose name was Horace, grumbled about the rain. He reckoned it was a real bugger. It'd keep away all the tourists, he said. He'd been making a bomb out of all the people showing up who had a fair few bob to spend. Then his wife Ailene caught Lubin's eye and cast her eyes at the ceiling. 'He's been going on like an old chook about that all day, mate,' she said. 'He thinks it should only rain in other dumps!' The pair of them laughed.

When Lubin said he didn't think he had enough money for all the food, they let him off. They even chucked in a few more things for a shout and said they'd make up a bill later on. Lubin was kept talking and was talked at for quite a while before he got away. No one else came into the shop while he was there. 'The blighters are probably all sleeping off the booze,' Horace told Lubin. 'The blasted motor camp's still full, there's even some flash poms here now, all the way from ruddy London. I don't reckon they have dolphins over there, ay!'

On the way back Lubin saw few people about. The rain had eased off, but the sky was still heavy with cloud. He didn't stop on the beach, weighed down as he was with the box of groceries. He spotted some blokes hanging about underneath the jetty. They were digging in the wet sand for shellfish. There was no sign that Opo was in the harbour. The sea looked dark and swollen.

11 Opo!

Effie wound up the gramophone and played the records while Lubin tinkered with the jalopy. 'We'll get it in the neck, we'll get caught if we stay on, Lubin,' Effie had told him while they ate. Both of them had been pretty hungry. Effie had cooked sausages in batter and fried bread. She'd wanted a hot meal she said, not cold mutton-bird. 'We went too far. We shouldn't have hid that body. We shouldn't have done it at all. Any day now we'll be copped, I'm certain. That man's going to find out! Why hasn't he showed up after Dorothy?'

Lubin tried to be patient with Effie. It wasn't like her to act so het up. Everything was getting Effie's back up. Saul Griff had become the threat she reckoned was lurking out there. She played the records and sang along with them at the top of her voice. It blotted out her thoughts, she told Lubin. Effie knew all the records off by heart now. She pretended she was Gracie Fields and lipped the words of 'Sing as We Go' over and over again. That cheered her up quite a bit.

Lubin went off to look for Pita after tinkering with the jalopy engine. 'It'll get us to Stewart Island once I'm finished,' he told Effie, grinning.

Effie didn't know where he'd got his knack for fixing engines. Adin had been useless at fixing anything. 'Don't be too long, son,' she said. 'I don't like being on my own now, ay.'

Lubin had no luck. There was still no sign of Pita anywhere. People were more keen to tell him that Opo had not been seen for a few days. Locals were getting a bit worried. Opo might have got crook. Some reckoned she had just pushed off to sea to look for other dolphins, that she wouldn't be back. Lubin gave up looking for Pita. He went back to Effie. No one had set eyes on Pita or his auntie for days either.

Effie stared at Lubin for a long time when he told her that Opo had also done a bunk, by the look of it, just like Pita and his auntie. 'Gladys and Ethel are clearing off,' she told him. 'They've had enough as well. Ethel didn't want to go, Gladys talked her into it. They're going to head south, where things are better and safer.'

Lubin knelt down beside Effie. She was sitting in the rocking-chair. He hugged her. He laid his head in her lap. Dorothy walked across and tried to push Lubin aside with her chest, treading on his legs.

'I'll track Pita down somehow, Mum. We can take him with us too when we leave. You don't want to leave without seeing him, do you?'

For a moment Effie covered her face. Then she whispered, 'I want us to take him with us, son.'

'Pita's almost your own,' Lubin said, looking up at her face.

'I know that. It makes it worse,' Effie said. But then she grinned and tapped Lubin on the nose. 'Pita would want to come with us, wouldn't he? If only we could find out where he is!'

While Lubin carried on for the rest of the morning working on the jalopy, Effie began to sort out what they could take with them. There didn't seem a lot she wanted to take. She reckoned they'd be better off making a new start by travelling light. They'd leave things, and memories, behind. 'The Evangelist will be watching over us, I'm certain,' Effie told Dorothy as she folded clothes into a suitcase. 'His soul isn't at Whangarei, Dot. It left before we did. He'll make certain we're all right. He can, from Heaven. Now the girls have shot through, there's only you left. We'll take you with us, don't you fret. We wouldn't leave you to starve like that nasty bloke. You're too precious.'

Dorothy stood shifting from one foot to the other. She swayed from side to side as Effie talked, then dug into her feathers with her beak.

'Hope you haven't picked up any fleas,' said Effie.

After another few digs Dorothy pooped on the floor. Ducking her head, Effie went to get the mop. Lubin was standing in the kitchen drinking milk. He grinned at her from ear to ear. 'I'm going to cadge some oil and petrol from the bowser,' he told Effie. 'The jalopy's ticking over like a bomb, but she's nearly empty. She'll be right enough soon!'

Effie rummaged about and found some money. She reckoned Lubin would be better off if he paid for the petrol and oil, so no one would get riled. 'We don't want too many getting het up. They'll be after us, we already owe the grocer,' she said. 'We don't even know the bowser man.'

Lubin hugged Effie before he rushed off to get a petrol can from a pile of cans behind the dunny. Both of them were a bit excited. Effie started to make some sandwiches. She gave Dorothy an extra feed. She switched on the oven and let Dorothy squat in front of it with her head stuck inside. Dorothy sprawled her long legs across the lino. 'We won't worry about the electric,' Effie said. 'We'll only be here for a bit longer. All we have to do is find Pita. Back on the road! You'll like it down in the south, Dot. There'll be loads to see and do. It's real pretty down there, not so many Nosy Parkers about. I've heard say the south has more sheep than people. We can find a bach miles away from people and have a good sort of life. A new start!'

It was a long time before Lubin came back. Effie had

121

begun to fret, looking down the road for him every five minutes. Lubin appeared carrying the can of petrol and some oil. Effie had put the sandwiches on to a plate. She had placed a candle on the table and had lit it, to celebrate. Dorothy stood up and turned round when Effie lit the candle. She was stretching out her neck, staring at the candle-flame. Dorothy didn't even shift when Lubin tore in from the back yard. He had to push her aside. His face was pale. He acted a bit shook. Effie saw straight off there was something wrong. All he said was 'I've got bad news.'

Effie drew up her hands.

'It's Opo, Mum,' Lubin carried on. 'She's dead. They've found her dead!'

Effie covered her face. Her heart had given a lurch. For a minute she'd thought Lubin had told her that Pita was dead.

Lubin sat down at the table. He seemed stonkered. 'An old Maori lady found her. They've had boats out all along the harbour, looking. The old lady came across Opo while she was looking for mussels at Koutu Point. Opo had got caught, Mum. They say she got stuck in the crevice of a pool when the tide went out. She was trapped there and died.'

Effie took Lubin's hands and clutched them. Lubin's hands were cold. They wouldn't stop shaking. 'Gentle dolphin meek and mild,' Effie whispered. 'Oh, the poor thing, the poor little tyke. It's a bad omen, Lubin, a real bad omen.'

'I went out to the farm too, Mum. I think Saul Griff's gone for good. The house is half-empty. I reckon he must have used that lorry to haul his things off after he'd shifted the animals. His stuff was still there when we rescued Dorothy. I reckon we're safe – I'm sure of it.'

They sat there but didn't touch the sandwiches that Effie had filled with Vegemite and lettuce. Dorothy was stretching out her neck more and more towards the candle-flame. Swaying from side to side, she shifted from one foot to the other. Her beak was almost in the flame. When Effie leant forward and blew the candle out, Dorothy pulled back her neck and head with a jerk. She twitched her feathers and shook herself. Then she pecked at Effie's hair.

'They're bringing Opo back here to the beach,' Lubin went on. 'There's loads of people down there. I reckon we should go down too, Mum. It'll be all right, it'll be safe.' Then he added, 'We could stay on for a few more days, ay, what do you think?'

Effie nodded. 'You're probably right, son,' she said. 'It'll give us a chance to find Pita.'

'They were going to build more rooms on to the hotel next month,' Lubin told Effie after they had sat in silence. 'Some bloke told me at the bowser. He reckoned Opononi would've become a real big tourist place.'

Effie watched Lubin's face. His lips trembled when he stopped talking. He'd always taken things to heart, she thought.

Effie packed the sandwiches into a paper bag in case they got hungry. They left Dorothy locked up in the kitchen with the blinds pulled down and set off to the beach in the late afternoon. All over the settlement there was a hush. There were no sounds of happy voices. Effie reckoned even the local seagulls must be keeping their beaks shut, it was so quiet. She worried aloud about Saul seeing them.

'It'll be all right. I told you, he's gone,' Lubin said. 'I'm certain.'

'I wish the girls were here,' Effie said. 'It's just you and me, son, like it was when we got here.'

'The Government passed a law this morning', Lubin told her as they crossed the road, 'to protect Opo or something. I heard some bloke saying. Bit bloody late now, ay, Mum? He said there'd been a friendly dolphin in the Cook Strait once who'd stayed there for over twenty years. No one touched that dolphin. Anyone who hurt Opo would've had to pay a big fine. They reckon someone might've killed her on purpose.'

Effie was looking up into Lubin's face, about to tell him off for swearing. But she could see how shaken he still was, so she kept her mouth shut. She felt a bit guilty. She didn't feel as stung by the news as Lubin did, but she did feel jittery. She was still thinking it could have been Pita who had been found dead. As they reached the beach she thought she saw Pita for a minute and nearly sang out. But it was just one of the other Maori boys, who were all over the show. There was a huge crowd gathered at the water's edge. They were staring out towards the sand-hills on the far side of the harbour. The sand-hills were already turning pink as the sun got lower in the sky. Behind them, the hotel had all its lights switched on. People were crowded on the veranda. They weren't talking. Maori ladies Effie had never seen before were standing out in the water. They had rolled up their frocks and were holding them high up their legs. They had waded out deep. No one was talking. Everyone just stood there, not moving. Soon the afternoon light began to wane as dusk drew closer. There was an eerie quiet. A couple of the ladies were crying into their hankies. Effie thought about going over to give them a hug. There was such a queer sadness all around them where they stood, a gloom that started to enter Effie's heart. Kiddies held hands as they waited and watched. Opo's body was being brought back by boat to this place where she had made people happy, where she had got strangers talking to each other and laughing together and sharing sandwiches. Slowly Effie couldn't help but be choked by the feeling around them. Saul Griff and all the rest of their worries seemed to fade just like the light was fading. Effie felt the loss. It reached out to her from the crowd standing so still. It reached out from the fretting kiddies. She held on to Lubin's arm as they stood beside a small group of kiddies. One of them, a little Maori girl, kept sniffing and rubbing her eyes. Effie reached over and took hold of her hand. The little girl moved closer. She leant against Effie's side without looking up.

As the dusk began to settle and the pink of the sand-hills slowly faded, a small boat appeared at the harbour mouth. It was heading in, chugging, towards where the crowd waited. Effie and Lubin moved forward with all the others. Still no one spoke. When Effie saw that tears were dripping from Lubin's eyes, she pulled him closer. She hugged the little girl to her with her other arm. The crowd on the shore moved together as the boat approached. The ladies out in the water were sobbing loudly now. Effie, too, started to cry. Through her tears she watched the tiny boat pulling Opo's body hitting the shore. It was hauled farther up on to the sand by a couple of burly blokes. The body was tied to the boat with rope. The blokes then untied the rope and dragged the body across the wet sand. Opo looked so small lying on her side, this creature who had become a national symbol of friendship and hope. No one moved. Each of them just stared at Opo. Each saw the wounds where the skin had been scraped off. She had struggled to escape from the crevice that had trapped her.

It was almost fully dark now. People started to murmur amongst themselves. One lady reckoned that this might not be Opo. It could be another dolphin, she said. Opo might still be out there, gambolling and frolicking, as happy as Larry in the sea. No one answered. No one believed her. The Opononi dolphin was dead.

The little Maori girl pulled away from Effie after a minute and disappeared into the crowd. Opo was dragged up on to the dry sand by a group of helpers. After a lot of talk and argument, her body was hung by rope from the lower branches of a pohutukawa tree. Effie shuddered as she watched this being done. 'That's cruel,' she whispered to Lubin. 'They shouldn't do that. They shouldn't hang her up, it's not right.'

Lubin stared at Effie without speaking. He had his arm round her. After a long time he said, 'It's all right, Mum. They have to decide what to do with the body. They'll probably find somewhere to dig a grave. They won't just leave her there. Everybody loved Opo.'

Effie didn't say any more. Lubin could feel her shaking.

A couple of the Maori ladies decided to sit with Opo's body beneath the tree until morning. Somebody brought down some candles and a torch from the hotel. Effie walked over and handed the ladies the bag of sandwiches. They nodded their thanks. Effie couldn't look at Opo hanging from the tree. She covered her eyes. Lubin took Effie by the arm. He led her home. The darkness that now covered the beach and the hotel had grown deeper. Cloud covered the moon.

In the days following, Opo was buried beside the Memorial Hall. There was talk, Lubin told Effie, that a monument was to be built. People could then come from all over to pay their respects there. Effie couldn't bear to go over to see the grave. She kept thinking about the grave she and Lubin had dug. She thought about it all the time. Her heart got stiff with guilt.

People were leaving, Lubin told her. They were packing up their tents, clearing out of the hotel, heading home with their caravans in their sadness. There was to be a memorial service. Lubin reckoned they should go to that.

'Yes, son,' Effie said, 'we must go. It's only right. We've a long road ahead, you and me. We've a lot to get through and make up for ourselves, I'm certain. I see that now, I see it. I think the Evangelist has been talking from above.'

Effie stared at Lubin. Lubin stared back. In Effie's eyes he saw the guilt that had entered there. He said nothing. He didn't know what the heck to say. Their clothes were packed up, Effie told him. They'd have to get going. It would only get worse. Saul Griff might not have gone for good. 'Why would he have pushed off like that? He had no reason. That's what I want to know,' Effie said. 'It says in the Bible, be sure your sins will find you out. We buried Mr Griff like they'll have buried Opo. But we showed no love for him. That's why we have such troubles. We're on our own again.'

'We've got Dorothy,' Lubin said.

'Yes, son,' said Effie. 'Dorothy's still with us.'

They hankered after leaving the next day, but they couldn't. Both of them felt too worn out. They had no energy and didn't want to clear off without seeing Pita. Effie still wanted Pita to go with them. She loved Pita now with all her heart. Lubin searched for him about the settlement, risking the chance of coming face to face with Saul Griff. Effie seemed so certain he'd be back, Lubin started to believe her. He didn't dare go out to the farm to have a look.

Telegrams and letters were arriving at the hotel when Lubin went over there. Some were addressed to the kiddies of Opononi. The messages of sympathy were being read out loud from the veranda every day. People stood about looking lost and fed up. A few blokes acted angry. They wanted revenge. No one was on the beach. The narrow strip of sand was deserted. Lilies had been laid along the water's edge. Opo's body had been photographed before it was buried and the photos were pinned on the hotel notice-board. One of the telegrams Lubin heard being read out had come from the Governor-General. Over all this the sun shone down with a fierce heat. Along the horizon, above the sand-hills on the far side of the harbour, lay streaks of cloud. It was so hot that even the breeze was scorching. Lubin sat on the beach alone. It was so quiet that even from there he could listen to the letters and telegrams being read out, over and over. Even the kiddies gathered on the hotel steps were quiet. They were listening too. No one came down on to the beach to join Lubin.

After a while he stood up and walked along the water's edge, away from the hotel. Along the shoreline lay piles of kelp and other smaller seaweed. Half-way along he came across a stranded jellyfish. Lubin prodded it with a stick. The jellyfish was bright red in colour. After staring at it Lubin backed off, feeling a bit sick. The jellyfish looked like a pool of blood lying on the white sand.

When he got to Pita's auntie's house Lubin stopped dead and stared. Then he hid behind bush. The front door of the house was wide open. A Maori lady he reckoned must be the auntie was sitting on the front step. He could hear voices coming from inside. The auntie didn't see Lubin. She was smoking a pipe and shelling peas into a big green bowl. Lubin was hidden from her sight by bush and by the car with no wheels, still parked in the drive. The sun shone right on to the front of the house. It reflected off the windows. The auntie's eyes were half shut. She didn't look up. From inside Lubin suddenly heard a voice. It sounded like Pita's voice, crying out something. Then there came a yell of pain and a crash. Lubin, crouched down behind a clump of toetoe, waited. The crying stopped. The auntie turned her head towards the door and yelled out, 'Tony, you screwy bastard, leave that boy alone or I'll brain you!' After a few more minutes the auntie got to her feet and went inside. She slammed the door shut behind her. Lubin heard shouts and then Pita's voice: 'It wasn't my fault, you buggers!' Then silence.

It got real quiet. Lubin stayed put. Nothing else

happened. Pita didn't appear. Lubin was certain it had been Pita calling out. When he heard some kiddies coming towards him along the path, Lubin got to his feet. In his lopsided way he ran back the way he had come, down along the beach past the hotel. He had to tell Effie straight away. He had left her all alone for too long. As he ran, he got shook with panic. Now he thought he could hear Effie's voice calling out. The voice was faint and he knew he was hearing it only inside his head, but it seemed so real. He fell over a few times before he had passed the hotel. Then Effie's voice stopped.

The first thing Lubin saw when he got to the bach were the smashed windows. There was no one around. Some of the window glass was lying amongst the weeds growing up the skirting. Lubin ran, yelling out Effie's name. The back door was wide open when he reached it. There was no sign of Effie in the kitchen. There was no sign of Dorothy. The windows at the back weren't smashed, but two of the kitchen chairs had been knocked over. Lubin raced through the rooms, but nothing looked out of place. Everything was quiet even after he yelled out Effie's name several times. Lubin shivered from fear and from shock. He kept calling out, back in the kitchen. When he stopped, he thought he heard Effie's voice. It was faint. It seemed to come from somewhere outside. Lubin pelted through the back doorway down into the yard.

Effie was in the dunny. She was holding the door shut with one hand. She held her head with the other. Blood was trickling down over her fingers. She was groggy. She stared up at Lubin, who looked scared stiff after he had managed to haul open the door. 'I'm all right, son, I bumped my bonce,' she said. She struggled to stand up.

Lubin leant down and picked her up in his arms. He hurried her back across the grass into the bach and laid her on the bed in her room. Effie's face was whiter than the sheets. 'It was him! He's pinched Dorothy back,' she whispered. 'He showed up just after you went, son. He must have been watching. He smashed the front windows first, so I just ran and hid. I told you he'd show up again!'

Lubin bathed the small cut on Effie's forehead. It had bled quite a bit. It wasn't a deep cut. It wouldn't need stitches, he reckoned. 'Did he do this?' Lubin asked.

'No, son, no, I only caught a glimpse of him before I ran. I tripped over on the step. He didn't do it. I was in such a silly panic. I should've stayed to fight.'

Lubin washed the blood from Effie's face and hair and gave her some aspirin crushed in honey.

'I'm a silly old sook, I could've tried to stop him. I peeked through the dunny door, son. He was dragging poor Dorothy off. Lubin, he was dragging her by her legs!' Effie burst into tears. She sobbed while Lubin held her until she'd calmed. 'I didn't think he'd spotted me,' she whispered. 'He didn't even look my way. But he yelled out that he'd come back! He was very drunk. He was soaked with booze, I'm certain.'

Lubin fetched a plaster from their medicine box and put it over Effie's wound. She had become sleepy from the shock. She lay on the bed without saying anything more. Lubin remained at her side. Slowly she fell into a deep sleep. As the afternoon wore on she started to snore.

12 Gathered by the Graveside

'Dorothy's dead, I'm certain,' Effie told Lubin the next morning. 'I feel it in my heart. That nasty bloke could've made another cloak out of her. I bet he's knocked off other emus too.'

Effie was sitting in her rocking-chair. She had got Lubin to shift it into the front room. She sat with her back to the smashed windows and stared at the wall as she rocked. Lubin had covered the windows with newspapers he had cadged from the hotel kitchen. In Effie's hands was a copy of *A Joy to Walk with Jesus*. Lubin stayed close to her after Effie had woken up properly.

They had decided to clear off tonight after dark, with or without Pita. Effie had slept the clock round, Lubin told her.

'I'm right as rain, son,' Effie said, grinning at him. She seemed pretty cheerful but was still a bit groggy.

'I reckon I'll go back out to the farm, Mum, before we leave,' Lubin said. 'Have a scout around. I feel like doing something to that creep. I'd bash his face in if he's still there. I could try to get Dorothy back.'

Effie's face twisted. 'No, son, you stay here by me, it's too risky. We've done enough. Vengeance never works. The authorities might get to hear what's been going on. We don't want to make things worse, do we?'

Late in the morning they visited Opo's grave. Effie had changed her mind about seeing it. She wanted to go now, as the memorial service was to be held there at lunch-

131

time. Lubin fretted that Effie wasn't well enough. She acted all right after he'd cooked her some scrambled eggs. They took it easy when they left the bach. They reckoned they'd be safe amongst the crowds which were bound to show up for the service. Now Saul Griff had Dorothy back, Effie said, he might stay clear.

A few people stared at the bandage which Lubin had tied round Effie's head. Ailene the grocer's wife was the only one who came up to speak. She spotted them and hurried over. She put her hand on Effie's arm and peered down into her face with a frown. 'Cripes, mate, you look like you've been knocked over by a bulldozer,' she said to Effie. Then she whispered to Lubin, 'Is she all right, Lube? She looks fair crook to me.'

'Oh, I just fell down!' Effie spouted brightly. 'Nothing broken, ay! My boy's a good nurse!'

'You look after yourself, Mrs. If you need any extras, sing out and I'll send the old boy over with some good grub. We can add it to your bill. My old boy's at home. He's as full as I don't know what, says it's because of the dead dolphin – but any excuse. Blokes love their booze, ay!' Then she laughed. Ailene carried on laughing as she went off towards the hotel. She was pulling a trolley. On it sat a box of meat pies. She was wearing men's trousers.

Effie whispered to Lubin that ladies shouldn't wear strides, it wasn't natural. 'She walks a bit like a man though, ay,' she added.

Opo's grave was heaped with flowers. There were bunches of gladioli, bunches of roses. There was even a huge bowl of cineraria, and daisy-chains which Effie reckoned the kiddies must have made. She had got Lubin to cut some flowering kowhai. They laid it on top of the small grave. Someone had made a wooden cross out of bamboo and hung up a sign. The sign read: *Here lies Opo the Dolphin, gay friend of all Opononi people and all the world.*

Effie knelt down on the earth. Clasping her hands she recited the Lord's Prayer. The hotel had organized the memorial service to be held at one o'clock. Already people were gathering outside the hotel. Some of them were making their way towards where Effie prayed. Seeing her there praying, some reckoned the service must have started. Lubin cast his eyes over the crowd. He saw no Pita, saw no Saul Griff. Effie had brought a scarf. Back on her feet she tied the scarf over her head, hiding the makeshift bandage. She kept her face lowered once the people had joined them. She and Lubin moved a little distance away. Lubin could see that the staring eyes were making Effie stiff with nerves. A few people nodded to Lubin in a friendly way. Most of them just looked sad and fed up. Few spoke to each other. Opo's special friend Lynette was there, in between her parents. Lynette was very pale. She wore sun-glasses. Her dad kept an arm around her shoulders. By one o'clock the graveside was chocka with mourners.

The kiddies who came, sat down in a circle round the grave. They joined hands. The Maori who had been the first to discover Opo was to be the main speaker. When Mr Hene began to speak they heard a gentle, sad voice. Effie lifted her head to look at him. He spoke first in Maori, then got them all to sing 'Now Is the Hour' before he carried on. The day was overcast. In the sky clouds were gathering, yet there was no breeze. The harbour water behind them was still. Up above seagulls hovered. To both Lubin and Effie the settlement had often seemed a secret, strange sort of place. It had a feeling of mystery about it. As she stood there Effie felt this more than she had ever felt it before. There was an atmosphere she couldn't get. She didn't understand it. She pressed closer to Lubin, listening to Mr Hene's gentle voice.

Mr Hene spoke of how he and his mates had found the orphan dolphin. Of how they eventually got the

133

message she was alone, that her mum had probably been shot by some thoughtless local bodgie. How Opo found friendship with the kiddies of Opononi, who soon flocked into the water to be close to her. Mr Hene named Lynette. He talked of Opo's special feeling for her, and about what had followed. People driving here from all over the country once the news spread. Hundreds of good people who wished to join in the fellowship and joy that Opo was bringing out in human hearts. The word spreading, reaching across the sea to Australia and beyond. People even showing up from America, to study and watch and to enjoy. Americans liked to be a part of everything, Mr Hene reckoned.

When he stopped talking, he nodded to a little Maori boy. The boy came forward, grinning from ear to ear. He looked pretty nervy and was lugging a huge wreath of lilies of the valley. He laid the wreath down on top of the grave, over the other flowers. Everyone sang a hymn. Then they were silent. Effie could hear prayers being whispered. Mr Hene stepped forward and put his hand on top of the Maori boy's head. He began to talk in a cracked voice about Opo's death. There were two versions, he said, about how Opo must have died. One of the versions was his own. He wished to speak of that too. It was thought by many that some bloke had been geligniting for fish in the place where Opo had been feeding that morning. That an explosion had stunned her badly and caused her to become stranded in the crevice where she had died. Some fool might have even done it on purpose, as Opo was taking all the fish. Some here reckoned they knew who that bloke was. Human greed was greater sometimes than love for wild creatures.

Mr Hene stopped speaking for a bit while he stared at people's faces. Lubin's face had gone pale as he had listened. Effie was staring up at him. When their eyes met, they both knew each other's thoughts. Saul Griff had fished that way. He had disappeared about the same time that Opo must have been dead. Effie could feel Lubin shaking. She took his hand in hers and held on tight.

Mr Hene cleared his throat. In his own humble opinion, he told the crowd, he didn't reckon this was how Opo had died. Their dolphin was a female dolphin. She was alone. She hadn't others of her own kind around her and she had sought them. Not knowing where to look, and finding only strange, human friends, she could not satisfy her need to reproduce. Breeding would have been her strength. It was her natural longing. This need was why she had liked to be stroked and touched like a child, for it was part of dolphin courtship. Opo had often turned over on her back to be stroked on her stomach. She had hoped, by doing so, that her new friends might give her what she needed. But in the end her urge to find a mate amongst her human friends became only a sadness for her. Her longing to reproduce was so strong, it could not be solved by these friends, who were not dolphins. And so, Mr Hene finished off saying, he believed that Opo had beached herself on purpose because she was not able to bring into her world another of her kind, a baby. She had killed herself in her despair.

When he stopped talking, Mr Hene hung his head. He covered his eyes for a moment, and when he drew his hands away he was weeping. The crowd was silent at what he had just told them. For a while there was no sound but Mr Hene's weeping.

Effie had started to cry. Her tears flowed silently down her cheeks. She let Lubin take her by the arm and lead her away from the crowd and the memorial service before it was over. Lubin held Effie to him as they walked along the road towards the bach. Effie didn't stop weeping. Lubin knew in his heart why Effie wept so bitterly. He knew without having to ask. He remembered the way

Effie had spoken about how she would never have kiddies of her own, how her face had looked then. Mr Hene's story had made the tears come.

All Effie wanted to do when they got indoors was to sit in her rocking-chair. Lubin crouched down beside her and laid his head in her lap. It had begun to drizzle with rain outdoors. A cold drizzle fell but it stopped very soon and the cloud drifted off. The sunlight came back, as strong as ever. But no brightness entered the room. The smashed windows, where Lubin had stuffed newspaper, locked out the sunlight.

Lubin kept looking up into Effie's face as she sat there. She remained very still for a long time. But then she looked down at him and smiled. 'I'm all right, son. I felt so torn at that service. That poor creature. Her life wasn't much chop, was it?'

'I love you, Mum. You know that, don't you? I'm your son,' Lubin told her.

'Oh, I know that, of course I do. You're a blessing.' Effie grinned. 'I bet you must be starving hungry. Come on, we'll have a good blow-out. It's nearly tea-time. There's sausages in the safe. And I'll cook a bread pudding – how about that?'

In the kitchen, while Lubin had a wash, Effie began belting out 'Beulah Land' at the top of her voice. When she stopped singing half-way through, Lubin rushed to see if she was all right. Effie was standing staring at the pots she had used for boiling rice. Her eyes were shining with tears. But through them she grinned at Lubin. 'I'm going to miss my dear girls, son,' she said. 'They haven't gone far off, I'm certain. I hear their voices, they speak to my heart. Ethel's egging us to carry on, and dear Glad will be spouting off a few prayers, bless her.'

After their tea of sausages and cabbage and kumara followed by the best bread pudding Lubin reckoned Effie had ever cooked, she said, 'I want to get back to Whangarei now, son. I want to see Dad. I want us to give him a decent burial, with a service. It won't be easy, I know. We'll have to sort things out with the authorities. Face up to the rest of it if we can. My mind won't rest until we do.'

'All right, Mum,' Lubin said quietly. He reached over and put his hand against her cheek.

Outside the kitchen window the afternoon sunlight was slowly dying. The silence that had come across the settlement after Opo had died was still there, though out in the bush birds were singing like billy-o.

'We can get a good night,' Lubin told Effie. 'Be bright and fresh for the morning, ay, Mum? We'll head off and go back if that's what you want.'

'I do want to sort it now, son. That service changed things for me. Maybe we'll find another Pita out there on the road one day. We found you, didn't we? We found you in the bush like tiny Moses. Perhaps there'll be a little Chinese tyke we can help. Gladys'd like that. She might come back and help sort things. I bet her and Ethel are knocking each other's blocks off by now with me not there to keep the peace!' Effie laughed, but stopped very soon. She covered her face with her hands. 'I don't reckon we'll see Dorothy again either,' she whispered.

They sat in the quiet of the kitchen. As the dusk came through the window, the birds in the bush stopped their song. It was a peaceful quiet that kept company with them. Holding hands they both felt the love that joined their hearts. They held on to that just as tightly. Effie talked in a whisper after a while. About days long gone, about the Evangelist, years before they knew he'd been a dark horse. Those days when they'd travelled the road with no money, but they'd a lot of laughs and good times. The Evangelist had sheltered Effie, and then Lubin, from the world. He'd protected them from all pain and sorrow. Though they hadn't known it then. Perhaps he

137

had betrayed them, Effie whispered to Lubin, by his doing that. They'd mucked up things here because he hadn't been with them. But they had loved each other all those years. That counted. It had been a good sort of life they'd had. Now it was up to the two of them to carry it on, start over once they'd sorted out their mistakes. And Lubin looked at Effie and saw that she'd never leave the Evangelist behind. She'd never toss away her memory of those days. The memories would keep her going.

'We can have a life on the road again, son, just you and me and the lamp-post, ay. But no preaching. I wanted to be a missionary once. All that's gone now, in the past. It went with your dad. We can't revive it, but we can get back on that road. One day soon we will, when it's all sorted.'

Effie was half asleep. Her head kept nodding. She'd jerk it up and grin at Lubin and repeat everything she'd already said. Lubin got up and lifted her into his arms. 'Giddy-up, gee-gee,' Effie said as Lubin carried her through to her bedroom.

As Lubin helped Effie undress, he tickled her. Effie started to giggle. She kept reaching down to slap him across the legs. Soon they were making a heck of a racket and laughing like billy-o when Effie's corset got stuck and she slipped down on to the floor. Lubin helped her up and gave her a big kiss on the lips.

Lubin had got Effie into her nightie. They had calmed down a bit. They were standing beside the bed and Lubin was brushing Effie's hair when Saul Griff smashed in the back door and barged into the kitchen. Effie let out an almighty shriek when he appeared at the bedroom doorway. Staggering from side to side he leered at Effie and then he leered at Lubin. In his hands he clutched a rifle. He stank of beer.

'Told you bastards I'd be back,' Saul Griff said, hawking on the floor.

13 Pita!

Lubin shoved Effie behind him. He stood facing Saul with as brave a face as he could muster. Saul Griff stared at them with his head lowered. He was showing the whites of his eyes. He stepped sideways, moving into the room. He held the rifle pointed towards them, began staggering up and down the space at the foot of the bed. Lubin held his hands behind his back. Taking hold of Effie's arm he pushed her slowly along the wall towards the covered-up window.

'What've you done with Dorothy?' Lubin shouted before Saul said anything else.

Saul just stared. He blinked. He was so drunk he had trouble focusing his eyes. 'Wouldn't you like to know. Don't get me riled, boy,' he said.

He carried on watching them before he spoke again.

'I felt real sorry for you pair of no-hopers. I knew all about your old man. He was a dud, a real shag artist. Came up here, making out he had religion. I sold him this place. We reckoned we knew what he wanted, my brother and me. We gave it to him. He wanted women and he got them.' Saul laughed. To Effie the laugh made the room get colder. 'I thought you two might've needed help. I was frigging wrong about that, wasn't I?'

Saul was edging forward, forcing Lubin and Effie back into the corner of the room. Saul staggered, then pulled himself up and tried to shove the rifle-barrel into Lubin's chest. His eyes narrowed to slits. He got so close to them they could smell his breath. Before he spoke again Lubin pushed at him, trying to grab the rifle. Saul stepped back, but he tripped over Effie's clothes which were strewn across the floor. He went sprawling, landing on his back. Without thinking, Lubin turned and grabbed Effie by the arm. Both of them tried to step across Saul, but Saul's hand jerked up and grabbed Lubin by the ankle. Lubin went sideways on to the bed, kicking out. Effie let out a yell as she was thrown off balance, but in a second Lubin was on his feet. In one movement he picked Effie up into his arms, barging forward, over the top of Saul, out of the room into the kitchen.

Saul was after them like a shot. He headed them off before they had reached the back door. He stood aiming the rifle at them. His eyes were bloodshot. They kept blinking. He was mumbling. 'Don't you give me any flaming acid, boy,' he told Lubin. 'I'm not out for it either, but don't push your luck. You tell me what's been going on. You'll know who my brother is, I reckon. That little Maori runt will've said. He blabs to everyone. I want the truth, savvy? I found my brother's bike down the road and thought that was pretty queer. Now I've found out that he hasn't been back to Whangarei. He hasn't been down there for weeks. I been checking. There and everywhere else.'

From his back pocket Saul drew out a small bottle of whisky. He downed half of it in one gulp, his eyes never leaving Effie and Lubin for a second. Then he added in a low voice, 'I heard all about you no-hopers. Half of Whangarei knows what you did down there. The cops are looking for you, I reckon. I've not let on to anyone where you are yet. Not until I get some facts.'

Lubin had slowly moved Effie to the far side of the kitchen and let her down. She was shaking all over. Saul stayed beside the door, his back to it.

'Why didn't you bring the cops?' Lubin said after a long silence.

140

Saul laughed. 'Don't want those bastards messing me up. You tell me, boy, I'm waiting. I'll wait all bloody night if I have to. I want the facts. You've been up to something in this frigging dump. My brother came here, I'm bloody sure. Where is he? You knocked him off just like you did your old man, ay?'

'Stop swearing in front of my mum, you slob. I'm not scared of you. Tell us what you've done with Dorothy!' Lubin shouted, trying to stop Effie taking in what Saul had just said.

Saul hawked on the floor. Effie had grabbed Lubin by the arm, trying to stop him shouting. Lubin stood up straight and stared Saul in the face. Saul raised the rifle. He aimed it straight at Lubin's chest. Lubin didn't move.

'I shot that bitch bird. What does it matter, I was going to anyway, she was a maniac. You cut out your cheek. I'm not frigging taking it from you, get me?'

Effie let out a muffled cry. Lubin glanced quickly at her. She had turned her back and covered her face with her hands.

'I don't believe you, you're talking rubbish,' said Lubin. 'You're so boozed up you can't even stand up straight. You stink like cow-poop.'

'Lubin – don't, son, please. We'll have to tell him!' Effie whispered.

Saul Griff took a few steps forward and a few steps back. He was trying to keep his balance. He took another swig of his whisky but then fumbled with the bottle and dropped it. He was shaking his head and blinking more than he had been before. His face had gone a deep red. He started fumbling with the rifle with both hands, trying to cock it. Lubin looked around for a weapon, yet he didn't feel as scared now. Saul was staggering all over the place until he held himself up by leaning against the wall near the doorway.

'I bet you killed Opo, you creep,' Lubin said in a low

141

voice.

Saul shuddered. 'Tell me what,' he mumbled. 'Tell me what.' He leant there, staring at them, his eyes half closed. The rifle began to slip from his hands. He looked as if he were going to drop the rifle, too, and pass out cold.

No one had noticed the little face at the window which had been peering in. They hadn't seen the little nose pressed up to the glass or the huge brown eyes that stared. Before any of them knew what was going on, a little figure came hurling into the kitchen through the open doorway. It screeched at the top of its voice. It held a shovel high up in the air. Lubin shouted, 'No, Pita, no!' The shovel bashed down on to Saul's head and Saul Griff fell. He collapsed on to the floor like dead mutton. He lay there not moving. He didn't make another sound.

Without even stopping to look at what he had done, Pita dropped the shovel and ran across the lino to Effie, throwing his arms about her. 'I bashed him, I bashed the bugger, I saved yous!' he sang out.

Effie held Pita in her arms, smothering him with kisses. Pita kissed her back, letting out little cries of shock. Lubin stepped over to where Saul lay. He knelt down and put his ear to Saul's chest. He couldn't hear any breathing. When he looked up, Effie was staring straight at him over Pita's shoulder. Lubin shook his head. Effie gasped. She hurried Pita off to the bedroom but came back after a minute. Lubin was still kneeling on the lino. 'I think he's a gonner!' he whispered.

Effie glanced over her shoulder towards the bedroom, then came farther into the room. 'We'll have to hide him, son,' she whispered. 'We can't let on to Pita, we can't! Do you want me to give you a hand? I've put Pita in my bed. He's freezing – he's shaking all over.'

'I'll get him outside,' Lubin whispered, staring at Saul. He picked up the rifle, holding it under his arm. Taking

Saul by the ankles, Lubin began to haul him across the floor.

Effie couldn't look. She turned her head away and then hurried back to the bedroom. Lubin heard Pita start talking to Effie as she went in, before the door was closed.

Slowly, Lubin pulled Saul across to the doorstep and down into the yard. He kept dropping the rifle. He stood for a minute getting his breath back before he carried on. Saul was a dead weight. Hauling him across the grass and reaching the dunny, Lubin pulled open the door with his foot. With a huge effort he shoved and heaved until Saul was propped up on the dunny seat. He threw in the rifle and pushed the door shut. Nothing could be seen from the outside.

Lubin couldn't face doing anything more. He ran back, hurtling into the kitchen to tell Effie what he had done. Pita was coming through from Effie's bedroom pulling Effie after him, singing out, 'I tells you, I got somebody outside, Missus Croft. You got to have a look!'

Effie had put on her dressing-gown. She was trying to grin. She stared at the shovel still on the floor, then looked long and hard at Lubin. Lubin nodded. Pita seemed to have forgotten all about Saul Griff. He led Effie by the hand through the doorway. Lubin followed. Pita pulled Effie down the steps and along the side of the bach, round the corner, and pointed. 'Look!' he shouted.

There on the earth crouched Dorothy. She was so bedraggled and soaking with wet and mud that Effie cried out and ran forward. Dorothy didn't stir. Her head was resting on the ground. Even in the dark they could see she was in a heck of a state. Her feathers were matted. Her legs were caked with mud. A length of old rope was twisted round her neck. Lubin and Effie managed to heave Dorothy up. They half carried her, half dragged her inside. While Effie switched on the oven, Lubin fetched some towels from the bathroom and began to rub Dorothy's feathers. He untied the rope and chucked it across the room.

Pita stood beaming in the middle of the floor. He had folded his arms. 'I saved her for yous,' he kept saying. then he added, 'I saw her at the farm. I been following that bugger tonight all over the place like a real pirate eye. He had her tied up in the shed. He'd hided her. I pinched her back for yous.'

Effie couldn't speak. She stood staring at Dorothy and then at Pita's beaming face, both hands over her mouth. Dorothy stayed where they had laid her. She seemed very weak. Lubin shifted her so that she was in front of the oven. Effie's face twisted with worry as she watched. Then she put on the jug for tea. Lubin carried on rubbing Dorothy dry. He scraped the mud off her legs.

They were sitting at the table an hour later when Dorothy perked up. She stood on her feet, shook herself, broke wind, and pooped on the lino. Then she started to dig in her feathers with her beak. Effie burst into a flood of tears.

'My auntie took me to see another auntie down the south,' Pita said after Effie asked him where he had been all this time. She had put Pita back into her bed and dressed him in her bedjacket. He was still shivery. Pita kept stroking the bedjacket. All over its front were furry pink pompoms. 'The other auntie's in a hospital. There was lotsa loonies – she's crook or somethink. A old pakeha man there told me he'd come from Mars. He stuck his leg out all the time and he gave me a pine-cone. He said it was worth lots. It came from Mars, too, he said. Look!' Pita pulled the pine-cone out of his pocket and held it up.

'When did you get back, Pita?' Effie asked.

'Coupla days ago, I think. Auntie's got another bloke now and he drived us in his Bentley. He's got a few bob, he's a wharfie from Wellington. He doesn't like kids much, he said they make him all cranky.'

'I was scared you didn't want to come and see me again,' Effie said. 'I really missed you, Pita.'

'I missed you too. I'd of come if I could've. I only got out tonight because Auntie's in bed with her bloke and they locked their bedroom door. She doesn't want me messing about with yous two. She thinks you're crackers.'

Effie grinned, hugging Pita to her. She had made another pot of tea. She and Lubin sat on the bed drinking it.

'They all reckon Saul Griff knocked off Opo when he was exploding fishes,' Pita confided to Effie. 'I heard my auntie say. She hates that Saul Griff now. She said people were out to get him. They sent the coppers out there to his farm after him. I didn't mind conking him. I reckon he was going to murder yous.' Then he put his mouth up to Lubin's ear and whispered, 'Will I get shoved in gaol? I think I killed the bugger. I'm real strong and it was a big conk.'

Lubin ruffled Pita's hair but didn't answer. He leant over and kissed Pita on the cheek. Then he hugged him. Lubin felt guilty. He'd been feeling angry at Pita, which wasn't fair.

Pita giggled. He rubbed his face. He hid his head under the bedclothes. 'That's dirty,' he said, still giggling. 'Blokes don't kiss other blokes.'

He carried on giggling when Lubin started to tickle him. When Effie joined in, Pita shook with laughter. He rolled all over the bed. They made so much noise, they didn't hear Dorothy. When they looked up, Dorothy was standing at the foot of the bed. Her neck was stretched out. Dorothy stared at them just like she had stared at

145

the candle-flame.

'Look at her,' said Effie. 'She's as thin as a rake.'

Lubin whispered to Effie that they had better tell Pita they were heading off in the morning. 'We can't take him now, Mum, it'd be too risky,' he said.

Effie nodded but she wouldn't look Lubin in the eye. After a minute she explained to Pita as best she could. She told him why he couldn't come. Pita sat up straight while he listened, looking first at Effie and then at Lubin. His eyes grew huge and dark as Effie talked. Effie told Pita everything. 'So we can't take you, Pita, you see. We'd be stealing you, and we might already be in trouble. You'd be missed. If you came with us, you'd be a part of what we've been up to,' Effie finished off. Her voice cracked. 'We'll be on the run, Pita. We might just head off down south now. The authorities'll be on our track for certain.'

'I don't care,' Pita answered. He was trying to look brave but his lips quivered. He hung his head. He was trying not to cry. 'I'm a part of yous now, Missus Croft. My auntie, she doesn't care. Her new bloke says I stink. Yous could hide me in the boot. I'd fit. I wouldn't tell on you or anythink.'

Effie reckoned her heart might burst when Pita looked into her face. She couldn't think what else to say to him. She looked over to Lubin but he had turned his head away. 'We'll decide in the morning then, ay,' she said in a shaky voice. 'We're all a bit too worn out. There's something Lubin and I have to do, Pita. How about you having a little sleep, ay?'

Lubin had slid off the bed. He went out to the kitchen, not looking at Effie.

'He's fast asleep, the little tyke's quite stonkered. He must have been wandering about half the night,' Effie said when she joined Lubin. 'What are we going to do, son?'

146

'Do you want us to take him?' Lubin asked her.

Effie nodded, but then she covered her face with her hands. 'I don't know, son, I don't know. I can't think straight,' she said.

'It'll get us into more trouble, Mum,' Lubin told her.

Effie looked up and moved over to the window. 'They all know, son, back in Whangarei. I heard what Saul said. Everyone knows about Dad.'

Dorothy had followed them. She stood on the cold lino, shifting from one foot to the other. She stared at the oven.

'I hate the thought of leaving Pita behind,' Effie added.

For a while neither of them could move. They stood there looking through the window into the deep darkness outside. Everything was still and quiet. They could hear the sound of sea. Far off in the distance a dog was barking. Lubin went over to Effie and put his arm around her. 'We'd better do something about Saul, Mum,' he said quietly.

'Yes, son, we better. Get it over with, ay. We'll have to hide him out in the bush.' She looked up into Lubin's face for a long time.

Effie lit the tilly-lamp. They pulled on their gumboots. Lubin carried the shovel. They went outside.

The dunny door stood wide open when they got to it. Saul Griff was nowhere in sight. The dunny was empty. The rifle had gone. They stood staring around them, scared stiff that Saul would suddenly rear up at them from out of the night. But nothing happened. All was quiet.

'I was sure he was dead, Mum. He wasn't breathing!' Lubin said.

'It's like Lazarus,' Effie whispered. After a minute she added, 'But where's he gone? That's what I want to know. I didn't hear a thing! Lubin, Lubin, we'll have to get away! He'll come back after us, I'm certain. He'll use

147

that gun!'

They stood facing one another. Above them the moon had come out from behind cloud. It was almost as bright as day. Effie clutched Lubin by the arm. Then, sensing danger all about them, they ran like the blazes across the grass to the bach.

14   Onward, Soldiers

Pita was telling Lubin for the third time how he'd been real brave like a grown-up Maori rescuing Dorothy from that pakeha crook Saul Griff. Every time Lubin looked down at the Maori boy, Pita's face was puckered. Effie and Lubin hadn't said anything about taking him, or leaving him behind. Lubin could hardly speak to Pita. Pita kept staring up into Lubin's face as they hurried to and from the jalopy carrying things. Half an hour had gone by. Pita had carried so much he was huffing and puffing like an old man.

'I saved the day for yous,' Pita said. 'That bugger must've dumped Dorothy, I think – ay, Lubin?'

Lubin was getting a bit fed up. Pita wouldn't leave him alone. He wouldn't stop chattering. Effie was having a lie-down before they faced going on the road. The shock of Saul Griff's being dead and then vanishing from the dunny had conked her out.

Effie tried not to think what might be waiting for them up ahead. Yet she reckoned they had just to clear out, push off. There was nothing else they could do. She wanted to keep out of Lubin's road as he packed the jalopy. And Pita's eyes had made Effie feel rotten in her heart, the look in them was too awful. But Pita couldn't be mixed up in it all. She had a little cry while she lay on the bed. She thought about Gladys and Ethel, about where they'd end up. It had all gone bung here, but there might still be a chance to win out if they sorted it. After doing that they might get freedom. They could get back

149

again into the gypsy life that Adin would've wanted them to have.

'I've made some tea, Mum, we're ready to push off.'

Lubin was in the doorway, Pita behind him, staring into the room. Effie struggled up and Lubin rushed to help her.

'What about that frock, Missus Croft?' Pita piped up, pointing at it.

Effie had hung up her best frock and hat on the door. She was wearing her old one for the trip.

'It's all right, Pita, I've still my toiletries to take out. I want to hang the frock in the jalopy. It creases if I don't hang it,' Effie told him. She couldn't look at Pita. She knew what the look on his face would do to her. Her heart lurched when he had spoken.

The three of them were quiet as they went out into the kitchen. Dorothy was sprawled in front of the oven. Effie had left the oven switched on.

'Dorothy's been good!' Pita told Effie. 'She hasn't done any jobs on the floor, I don't think. I'se been working hard getting your stuff in your car. I'm a real man at getting things done in the house, my mum told me once. I'se a real credit, she said, loadsa times.'

They were sitting at the table. Effie put her hands up over her face and held them there. Lubin poured the tea. Pita started to sniff, wiping his nose on his sleeve. After a minute he got down from his chair and walked slowly out of the kitchen, his head hanging. Effie and Lubin heard him going into the bathroom. He had often done that. He liked to wash his hands and face with Effie's lavender soap. He liked the smell of it. Effie couldn't look at Lubin. She drank her tea. They sat in silence for a while until Pita had been gone for several minutes. They hadn't heard him come out of the bathroom. The bach was still and quiet. There were no sounds from outside. It was now dead of night. Effie reached over and took hold of Lubin's hand. Dorothy hadn't stirred. 'It's time to get cracking,' Effie whispered, 'or we'll get caught.'

They didn't notice Pita straight off. He just appeared in the doorway and stood staring at them. When Effie looked up and glanced over she got a heck of a fright. She nearly yelled out. She thought one of the girls had showed up. Pita stood there grinning at them shyly, his hands behind his back. He looked almost like somebody else. He had plastered his face with Effie's talcum powder and put on Effie's best frock. The frock fitted him perfectly. With his long black hair, and Effie's feathered hat perched on his head, he looked like a tiny lady.

For a minute no one could speak. Then Pita said, 'No one'd know who I is now, Missus Croft. I could be one of your ladies, lotsa peoples know about them. I told people they was real.' He walked into the kitchen swaying his hips and holding his head up high. 'Yous could take me now! No one would see it was just me!'

Effie started to grin, but then she burst into tears. Lubin looked at Pita with his mouth open. Dorothy suddenly got to her feet. She stood very still, staring at Pita. Pita ran to Effie and Effie hugged him to her, kissing his face and getting powder all over her lips. 'Bags I come, bags I come, please. I'd fit in!' Pita cried out.

A little while later Effie stood in the front room, alone with Dorothy. Lubin had made a halter for Dorothy. She stayed close to Effie's side. Lubin and Pita were already out in the jalopy. 'We're heading off now, Adin. I hope you can hear me,' Effie whispered. 'We're taking Pita after all. The little tyke got so frantic, he put on my best frock as a disguise so we might take him.'

Effie felt quite cheerful as she hurried out through the kitchen into the yard, pulling Dorothy with her. Across the frosty grass the dunny door still stood wide open.

The night was pretty cold. A wind had sprung up. She could hear the jalopy ticking over, and almost ran to the front of the bach. Lubin was there waiting. It was a real tight squeeze, but they got Dorothy into the back of the jalopy, on the floor. There was just enough room for Effie on the back seat, next to luggage and pots and boxes that were piled up. Pita was still wearing Effie's frock. He sat up straight in the front seat grinning shyly. Effie hadn't had the heart to make him take the frock off.

Lubin steered the jalopy out on to the road. Dorothy kept shifting around at Effie's feet. She finally squatted down and rested her head on Effie's lap. As they set off, Pita turned his head and grinned from ear to ear at Effie. 'Bet yous glad I'se coming,' he said.

Effie just nodded and grinned. She was a bit too choked to speak. She'd wanted to leave a note for Pita's auntie. Lubin had reckoned they'd better not. There wasn't time. They could send a letter from Whangarei or telephone a message to the hotel.

They left Opononi behind pretty quickly, though Effie had asked Lubin to stop at Opo's grave. She got out with Dorothy to place copies of Adin's tract in amongst the flowers. Fresh flowers had arrived every day from all over the country, sent by people who mourned Opo's death. Effie recited the Lord's Prayer before she went back to the jalopy. She was a bit riled about not bringing any flowers herself. Dorothy stood beside Effie twitching her feathers.

Lubin made certain he didn't drive past the farmhouse. He took a side-road that shook the jalopy so much he was worried sick about possible damage. The side-road was full of pot-holes. By the time they got back on the main route, he was having trouble with the steering. He didn't let on, and Pita and Effie didn't notice.

Pita wouldn't stop chattering even now they'd got away. 'I'se getting good learning,' he was saying as they careered along, heading south. 'I'll be a proper pirate eye when I get big and sort things for us and I can wear stuff like this frock so no one'll spot me. I'll work real hard for yous and we'll make a bomb. We can buy a flash house, ay, Missus Croft, with a big back yard for Dorothy.'

He stopped talking for a breather. Lubin turned his head to see if Effie was all right. She grinned at him, but they didn't speak.

Lubin looked worn out, Effie thought. They'd have to stop for a cuppa along the road, somewhere safe. She'd made tea in Adin's old thermos and brought food. There'd been a few fly cemeteries left she'd kept in the safe with some stale biscuits. Lubin would have to stop anyway, to study the road map. It seemed a long road ahead. She hoped the money they had left would last. The jalopy soaked up petrol like water, Lubin had told her.

Pita sensed that Lubin and Effie's nerves weren't too good. Lubin had glared at him. He stayed quiet now. No one even laughed when Dorothy broke wind loudly. Lubin just wound his window down and the pong went away. Dorothy was acting fidgety. Effie wondered if there was something the matter with her. Dorothy should have been as worn out as they were, Effie reckoned. She must have had a rough time of it, out at the farm tied up like a trussed chook. Dorothy kept trying to stand up and sit down. She scratched Effie's legs with her big feet. She kept shaking her bottom. It was pretty cramped for all of them.

Effie sat trying to face the future in her thoughts. She thought about Adin, about how much she still loved him. It was all over for them now, she reckoned, unless they got a bit lucky. Pita had fallen asleep. Effie's hat had slipped off his head. In the quiet, Effie began to feel a bit racked with nerves. 'Lubin, son?' she whispered.

Lubin glanced back at her. 'I know, Mum,' he whispered back. 'It's all right. I feel the same. We'll be all right.'

153

Lubin was still having trouble with the steering. He tried to pretend there was nothing wrong and gave Effie a sort of grin, which made her feel worse.

Outside the jalopy the wind blew stronger. Rain began to fall. The rain beat against the windows. The windscreen-wipers worked in slow motion and thunder sounded, coming closer. Lightning flashed, lighting up bush on either side of them. Effie could smell the dampness creeping in. Lubin had wound up his window and the jalopy had warmed a bit. Effie began to nod off despite feeling nervy. She had pulled the blanket around her tightly. Dorothy had moved and was now sitting half on Effie's lap. Her neck and head rested across Effie's shoulder. The warmth from Dorothy's body made Effie even more sleepy. Now it was bucketing down with rain. Lubin was leaning forward in his seat, his face pressed up against the windscreen. He couldn't figure out if they were still on the same road. He couldn't see more than a few feet in front. Before long he was the only one awake.

When the jalopy crashed off the road into a ditch, the storm was reaching its peak. Lubin had fallen asleep at the wheel. Effie had been snoring. She and Lubin woke up and yelled out in fright when they felt themselves being tipped over. The jalopy's near-side wheels had run off the edge of the road. The huge jolt caused the luggage to fall all over the show. Effie started yelling. Lubin yelled out too, but there wasn't a sound from Pita until he started to whimper. Effie couldn't move. Dorothy lay on top of her, struggling like billy-o. Effie screamed as she felt sharp, tearing pains in her legs, until they went numb. Most of the boxes beside her had been thrown down across her legs.

Lubin was first out of the jalopy. He climbed up through the driver's door, pulling Pita with him by the arms, dragging him away from the ditch. Pita seemed unhurt, he was still half asleep. Lubin ran back and got Dorothy out. Then he lifted the boxes off Effie's legs where they had trapped her. Effie had passed out cold.

It took Lubin quite a while to free Effie. Pita yelled out that he would run and find help. Dorothy had scrambled clear and was on top of the bank.

'You stay there! Get hold of Dorothy!' Lubin yelled to Pita above the sound of the rain. He picked Effie up after freeing her, easing her out through the front over the backs of the front seats, then carrying her up the bank. Across the road stood a group of trees close together. He carried her there, Pita following, dragging Dorothy. Lubin laid Effie on a carpet of moss beneath one of the trees. He then ran back to the jalopy and fetched blankets. He shut the open door so no rain would get inside. He quickly checked over the underside of the jalopy before hurrying back to the others.

Pita was shaking. His teeth chattered. Dorothy acted all right, Effie having cushioned her from the crash. Lubin quickly looked Dorothy over with the torch. There were a few cuts on her legs, and she stood shaking herself and twitching her feathers. She was stamping on the ground with her right leg and twisting about trying to push her beak up her bottom. Pita had tied her to a low branch.

'You all right, Pita?' Lubin yelled. The falling rain was so loud he didn't hear Pita's answer.

Pita was staring at Effie. Effie lay very still. Her face was drained of blood. Lubin had folded one blanket round her tightly, with the other one underneath. Above them forked lightning lit up the sky. No other cars had passed along the road since the crash. Lubin reckoned he'd taken a wrong turning and they were lost. It didn't look like it was the main road they were on now. Lubin shouted at Pita to go back and get the thermos of tea and the food from the jalopy. Pita ran. He was crying his eyes out. He left the jalopy door open as he turned to come back, and Lubin yelled at him so roughly Pita dropped the thermos. He looked pretty wretched. Lubin gave him a hug. The frock Pita wore was drenched. It clung to him and the powder on his face was streaked.

Together, with Dorothy standing over them, they crouched by Effie's side beneath the trees. Lubin rubbed Effie's arms through the blanket. He tried to get her warm. The rain was easing off. The storm seemed to be getting a bit quieter.

'Is your car all right?' Pita yelled out.

'The back axle's busted!' Lubin yelled back. 'It's a write-off! I'll go for help soon!'

When Effie came to, she was quiet. She grinned weakly. She stared at Lubin and then at Pita as if she wasn't certain who they were. After a few minutes her face twisted. She said she couldn't feel her legs. She started to struggle up to have a look. 'They aren't there, son. They're not there!' she cried out.

Lubin helped her to sit up and showed her that her legs were all right. They weren't cut but they were badly bruised. Lubin hugged her. Pita pulled Dorothy closer so that Effie could see her. Dorothy plonked herself down on to the moss beside Effie. She was quieter now and didn't fidget. Lubin had untied the halter lead. The rain was easing off. The storm was passing. Raindrops dripped down from the leafy branches above them. Lubin had brought over Effie's brolly and, opening it, wedged it into the branches above her. The moss had stayed dry.

'Mum, the jalopy's wrecked. I'll have to go and find someone. There's probably a farm down the road. Can you try to stand up? I'll help you.'

Lubin managed to get Effie almost on her feet, but her legs gave out totally. He lowered her back on to the blanket and she lay there with her head resting against the tree-trunk.

'I can't feel my legs, son, they're numb,' Effie said. 'They don't hurt now, though.'

After Lubin had lowered her down, Effie covered her face with her hands. 'We're done for, son. It's all over,' she whispered. She peered up into Lubin's face.

Lubin couldn't speak.

'We'll be right Missus Croft, you better not worry,' Pita piped up. 'I can piggyback you down the road, I think. We can find a farm bloke and he can come back and get our stuff for us. We can all go for help!'

Effie looked at Pita. She couldn't help grinning a bit. Pita looked so dippy. Most of the talcum powder was washed off his face but it was streaked with white. The frock had shrunk in the rain, it was about six inches shorter. Pita had put the hat on again. It was sopping wet and flopped down over the back of his neck.

'You'd best get some warm clothes on Pita, son,' Effie said. 'Lubin, get him your old raincoat. He's covered with goose-pimples. Look at him.'

'You called me son,' said Pita, grinning at Effie.

Quite soon Pita sat against one of the trees, buried in the raincoat. They drank tea from the thermos and shared the fly cemeteries. Above them the sky was clearing. The lightning and thunder were now farther off. They were on the verge of a huge area of native bush. Around them were pongas and huge kauri trees which towered over them. The undergrowth was choked with bracken and king fern.

'We might spot some kiwis if we're lucky, ay,' Pita was saying, stuffing a bit of fly cemetery into his mouth. 'Dorothy'd like that, she must get homesick for other birds. We'd have to get quiet, though.'

After talking on and on, Pita became quiet. Dorothy kept standing up, shaking her bottom, then sitting down again. Pita fell asleep, his head resting on a tree root.

'It's the shock,' Effie whispered, staring over at him.

157

'I don't feel so good, Lubin,' Effie whispered after a while. 'My legs feel like they've been through the wringer, the nerves are shot. I still can't move them. My chest hurts, son. It hurts a lot.'

'I'll go and get help in a bit, Mum. There'll be someone along the road. Try not to worry. We can get them to telephone a doctor. People'll help.'

'I got so confused in the jalopy, son. One minute there I was all for us just tearing on south and not stopping. I reckon the crash has told us we have to get to Whangarei, sort everything out. It won't be easy, I know. The crash was an omen, Lubin.' When Lubin stayed silent she added, 'I was thinking of your dad so much when we set out. You know, son, he never took all that preaching on the road serious. I've always known that. He just pretended. He wanted the money. He was a real character, Lubin, a real dark horse. I can see him in Pita now. Pita was sent to us, just like you were sent. I see your dad in Pita's eyes, he has Dad's grin. Pita's here to make things better for us, I'm certain.'

Dorothy had moved closer to Effie. She pushed herself up against Effie's side and hadn't stood up for a good five minutes. She was staring into the bush.

'Dorothy's real warm, Lubin. She's just like a hotty,' Effie whispered.

Above them, as the sky slowly started to clear, the moon was coming out. It didn't seem to be so dark. They had been quiet for a while when Effie suddenly looked frantic. She turned her head in the direction Dorothy was staring. 'I can hear someone coming, Lubin!' she whispered. 'There's somebody out there in the bush. It might be Saul Griff after us with that gun. Listen!'

Lubin peered about him. He couldn't see or hear anybody. Effie had twisted about and was staring towards a clearing on the far side of the rise they were sitting on. Lubin glanced at Effie's face after searching the bush with his eyes. Effie looked scared stiff for a minute, but then her face began to break into a huge grin.

'I can see Gladys, Lubin! It's Gladys, and there's Ethel!' Effie cried out. In her mind's eye she could see the girls tramping towards her along a path in the bracken. Their arms were outstretched and smiles of greeting were on their faces. They were sopping wet.

Pita woke up at Effie's cry.

'Look, Pita, look who's coming. It's the girls!' Effie sang out.

Pita rubbed his eyes as he looked to where Effie was pointing. After a long silence he yelled, 'I sees them, I sees them, Missus Croft. Theys come to rescue us!'

Lubin sat there grinning from ear to ear, looking from Effie's face to Pita's. Pita got up and ran off towards the jalopy. Effie held up her arms towards her girls as they tramped closer.

In a minute Pita came running back lugging the gramophone and a record. 'It still works, I think!' he called out as he ran. He put the gramophone beside Effie on the earth and wound up the motor, inserting a needle while Lubin shone the torch.

Effie was already yacking away to the girls. She yacked about her dud legs and the crash and their having to get to Whangarei, as the music began. Gracie Fields's voice belted out 'Sing as We Go', and the song sounded louder than they had ever heard it before. Pita stood there beaming, with his arms folded. Then he started to dance. He swung his arms out and twirled about, trying to sing along with the words. Lubin stared at Pita with his mouth open. 'Look, Missus Croft, look at me. I'se a dancer!' Pita called out.

Effie was reaching out to hug Gladys when Dorothy suddenly lurched to her feet as if she were drunk. Swaying from side to side Dorothy shook herself and broke wind so loudly they heard it above the music. Then she

159

squatted. From out of her, as she grunted and strained, came a huge egg. Once it hit the ground the egg rolled a bit before it came to rest against Effie's feet. Dorothy stood up. She stretched up her neck and head and peered down at the egg with a snooty look. As the song from the gramophone came to an end and Pita stopped dancing, they each became still, staring at the egg.

'See, can you see?' Effie cried. 'It's another omen! It's a sign for us, a sign of a new start!'

Effie picked up the egg. She wiped it clean on her frock and kissed it. After a minute she placed it back on to the moss. For a while she cushioned it with her hands. Then she said softly, 'I always knew Dorothy was a godsend. We're going to be all right back in Whangarei, I'm certain. I feel it in my blood. His eye is on us sparrows.' And she looked over to where she could see Ethel, and grinned.

In the next few hours Lubin couldn't leave to go to look for help. He wanted to make sure that Effie would be all right. He reckoned he could wait until the night had gone. After each of them had rested, Lubin and Pita moved over to where Effie lay on the blanket. They knelt down and put their arms around her. Effie hugged them back. She was gazing up into the faces of her girls and on her face there was a look of joy. After a minute Pita started tickling Effie. Lubin joined in and tickled Pita. Soon the three of them were trying to tickle each other. They began laughing out loud when Dorothy suddenly shot off. She lurched away from them and ran round and round in circles and leapt into the air.

'Full of the joys of life!' Effie sang out.

Up above them in the sky, the rain clouds were now gone. The thunder and lightning had gone. And down through the trees, as they waited there for the dawn, bright silver light from the moon came streaming.